Under My Roof
Nick Mamatas

Under my roof

ISBN: 1-933368-43-8

ISBN-13: 978-1-933368-43-6

©2007 Nick Mamatas

Cover Design by Tim Goodman

Text Design by Luke Gerwe

Published by Soft Skull Press

55 Washington Street, Suite 804

Brooklyn, NY 11201

www.softskull.com

Distributed by Publishers Group West • www.pgw.com

1 800 788 3123

Printed in Canada

Cataloging-in-Publication data for this title is available from the Library of Congress.

To Hannah Wolf Bowen and Sophia Jordan Cully.
Thanks for all you have done and all you will do.

Every normal man must be tempted at times to spit on his hands, hoist the black flag, and begin to slit throats.

—H.L. Mencken

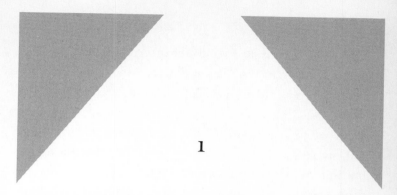

1

My name is Herbert Weinberg. I know what you're thinking. *That sounds like an old man's name.* It does. But I'm twelve years old. And I know what you're thinking.

In fact, I'm sending you a telepathic message right now.

Yes, it's about the war. And yes, it is about Weinbergia, the country my father Daniel founded in our front yard. And yes, I have been missing for a while, but I'm nearly ready to go back home.

But I'll need your help. Let me tell you the story.

It was Patriot Day, last year, when Dad really went nuts. Thoughts were heavy like fog. Not only was everyone in little Port Jameson remembering 9/11, they were remembering where they were on September 11th, 2002, September 11th, 2005, 2008, on and on. The attacks were long enough ago that the networks had received a ton of letters and email demanding that they finally re-air the footage of the planes slicing through the second tower, because nobody wanted to forget. Schools took the day off. Banks closed. Some cities set up big screens in public parks to show the attacks. I was excited to finally see the explosions myself. Nobody else could really picture them properly anymore. I drew a picture in my diary.

My mother Geri had forgotten pretty much everything except how beige her coffee was that day. She had been pouring cream into her blue paper cup when she looked up out of the window of the diner and saw the black smoke downtown, and she had just kept pouring till it spilled over the brim. She found my father later that day and told him that they were going to move to Long Island immediately.

And they did. Every year since she forgot a little bit about that day. What was the name of the diner? Did she order a bagel with lox or just the coffee? Did she think it was Arabs or did the liberal centers of her cerebellum kick in to say "No no no it could have been anybody"? Did she want to kill someone? Drop an A-bomb on the entire Middle East? She didn't know anymore. All she remembered, and all I plucked out of her head, was her off-white coffee.

My father Daniel, on the other hand, didn't remember anything but the nuclear weapons. Dirty bombs, WMDs, suitcases filled with high-tech stuff; that was all he could think about. He took a job mopping floors at SUNY Riverhead so he could take classes for free. Physics. Mechanical engineering. His head was like an MTV video—all equations, blueprints, mushroom clouds, people running through the streets, and naked ladies, in and out—flipping from image to image. With every war Daniel got more frantic. The President would say some stuff about not ruling out nuclear weapons, and I could tell he wasn't kidding. My father would stay up all night, just walking around the dark kitchen and smacking his fist against the table. On the news, they kept showing more and more countries on a big map, painted red for evil. All of Latin America was red now and even the normal people in

California died when someone ran the border with a bomb or shot down a plane over a neighborhood.

Dad read the newspapers, spent whole days in the library and all night on the computer. He was getting fat and losing his hair. He was a real nerd though, so nobody really noticed that he was slowly going mad. Actually, the problem was that he was going mad more slowly and in the opposite direction from everybody else. At night he dreamed of being stuck on an ice floe or on the wrong side of a shattered suspension bridge. Mom and I would be drifting off to sea on another ice floe or sliced in half by snapping steel cables. Then Dad would see the ghosts of firefighters and cops, white faces with no eyes, and they would point and laugh.

So Daniel studied. Researched. Thought of a way out.

Dad waited until I was out of school for the summer to make his big move, because he knew I would make a good assistant. He was laid off by SUNY because of budget cuts—Mom blamed his erratic behavior, but Daniel wasn't really any more eccentric than his other co-workers. He sold our nice car and bought a ratty old station wagon, and spent all day tooling around in it, while Geri clipped coupons and made us tuna fish with lots of mayonnaise for dinner. They didn't send me to genius camp that summer (I'm not really a genius, I just know what smart people are thinking) so that's how I ended up being Prince Herbert I of Weinbergia.

Dad woke me early one hot day, just as the sun was rising. He looked rumpled, but was really excited, almost twitching. I half expected to see a little neon sign blinking *Krazy! Krazy! Krazy!* on his big forehead like I did back when Lunch

Lady Maribeth went nuts and started throwing pudding at school, but he was actually normal.

"C'mon Lovebug, I need your help," he said, shaking my ankle. He hadn't called me Lovebug since fourth grade, and his mind was going three thousand miles an hour, so I didn't know what he wanted.

"What is it?"

"We're going to the dump to look for cool stuff. C'mon, we'll get waffles at the diner on the way back."

I always wanted to go to the dump and look for cool stuff. I was really hoping to find something good like a big stuffed moose head or a highway traffic sign, but then in the car Dad told me that we were going to look for the ingredient that made America great.

"In fact, they call it Americium-241. It was isolated by the Manhattan Project, Herbert." Daniel loved to talk about the Manhattan Project.

"I don't think we're going to find that stuff at the dump, Dad."

"Smoke detectors, son. Most smoke detectors contain about half a gram of Americium-241," he said with the sort of dad-ly smile you usually just see on TV commercials.

"How many grams do you want?"

"Well, 750 grams is necessary to achieve critical mass, but we'll want more than that to get a bigger boom," he said. He was thinking about turning on his blinker and how much smoother the ride in the old car was, not about blowing anything up. "I guess we'll need about 5000 smoke detectors."

"Uh..."

"Don't worry. I don't plan on finding all of them today."

He pulled the car into the dump and gave me a pair of gloves and a garbage bag. It was still early morning so the dump hadn't started getting hot and stinky yet. Dad let me go off on my own too, so we could cover more ground. I bet Mom or a social worker would have complained that Dad wasn't worried enough about my safety, but really, he was. As far as he was concerned, the safest place in the world was in a garbage dump, digging around for radioactive smoke detectors.

There wasn't all that much cool stuff at the dump, mostly just big bags of rotting food and milk containers, and broken Barbie Dream Houses—lots of those for some reason. There were old computers too. I liked checking out the motherboards and the stickers the college kids plastered on the side of their old monitors, but I couldn't find any moose heads or old hockey sticks or valuable comic books that some angry mother threw out or any smoke detectors. Mostly, people just leave them up on the wall, even if they don't work anymore.

I was playing around in this neat car I found that had a steering wheel that still moved around when Dad came running up with his own garbage bag. He'd found like twenty. "How many ya get, Lovebug?" he asked, then he frowned and mentally counted to ten when he saw the empty bag next to me. "Herbie, we really need to find these materials. Did you even look?!"

I shrugged. "It's hard. What do you want me to do? I can't look everywhere all at once."

He waved me out of the car. "C'mon. You just have to go about it systematically." He walked to the closest pile of garbage and then started going through it, one bag at a time. We poured through all the bags in one pile, tossing aside the smaller white plastic bags full of disgusting toilet paper, cardboard boxes with pictures of lasagna and fried chicken on them, newspapers from last week with headlines about the White Menace (Canada), gloppy leftover food mess sprinkled with white maggots, and all sorts of other junk. And then I found a smoke detector, at the top of the tenth bag we opened. Daniel gave me a big hug for that. "Now you can do the rest of this pile yourself. I'll be in that quadrant over there." Saying "quadrant" made him feel military.

Long Islanders are pigs. I found another smoke detector in the middle of a greasy pound of red spaghetti, but that was it. Everything else was just gross, from the moldy bathroom rugs to little baby clothes smeared in grease. Dad found me a bit later, his bag a little fuller. "Scored twelve all together. Let's get home, quickly now."

And that's what we did every morning. There was new garbage every day, plus there was always a chance we had missed something. Daniel printed out a list of things that might have some Americium-241 in them. Smoke detectors, and some medical testing equipment, and moisture density gauges all use the stuff.

"You know what a moisture density gauge looks like, Lovebug?" Dad asked me one morning.

I read his mind, then told him.

"You're such a smart boy."

We didn't find any moisture density gauges at the dump, but we did find some cool-looking stuff from the public hospital. They'd lost beds due to budget cuts. As the days wore on, we had more competition in the dump. Daniel was the only one after smoke detectors, but some poor people were spending their days at the dump, looking for old shoes or funny lamps or computer monitors to sell on eBay. I saw one guy cart away a giant bag full of stiff old bagels. Even he didn't know what he was planning on doing with them, but I could just picture his family in a dumpy living room: the kids all had dirty faces and crooked teeth, their little fists wrapped around mismatched forks and knives, and they wore white napkins around their necks like bibs. Then their dad would walk in and pour all the bagels onto the middle of the door he had put up on sawhorses to use as a table, and they'd all dive in at once, screaming, "FOOD!" It was so funny.

One of the poor people got really upset because he was poor and took it out on me, yelling and screaming that I was stealing garbage from his spot. Daniel came running, ready to tackle the guy but stopped, frozen with fear, when the poor guy picked up a rusty muffler and swung it over his head. "I'm a workin' man!" he shouted, "I'm working here in the dump, trying to get some food for my family." Inside his mind I could see him turning over, going from normal to crazy. The dump guys finally came out of the trailer where they watch TV all day with some crowbars to chase him off.

Most of the poor people were normal though. They were used to being poor, but just started coming to the dump because they had gotten poorer after the taxes went up or after they lost their job at a gas station. The worst poor people were the ones who used to have money. They really went crazy. I hoped that after Daniel became afraid we'd stop going to the dump, but he really wanted that Americium-241. We just went earlier in the day, while the poor people were still asleep on their couches, dreaming along with an infomercial or the national anthem on TV. It was fine after that, except for one time a black lady yelled at me for stepping on a pie plate she thought was a collector's item.

It took all month to get 5000 smoke detectors, plus a few things from the hospital. Daniel spread them out over the basement and put me to work plucking the little silver bit of Americium-241 out of each of the detectors. I wore a nose mask that Daniel wasn't sure would work, rubber gloves, a smock. I used tweezers and a big magnifying glass connected to the table. Daniel worked on the other end of the basement—we kept the material in different piles so it wouldn't achieve critical mass and kill us.

The day Geri was laid off she nearly found out what were up to. Her sadness and anger preceded her into the driveway by nearly a minute, so I told Dad that I heard the car and we rushed upstairs, just in time to slam the door to the basement behind us and nonchalantly stand in front of it, while still wearing our masks and smocks.

"Hi boys," Mom said. She carried a cardboard box fill of little doodads from her cubicle with her. A frame with a picture of me from the two weeks I was in Little League stuck out of the top. Her misery evaporated as she took us in. "What are you two doing?"

"Ships in bottles!" Dad said.

"Model trains!" I said, because that is what Dad was thinking right before he changed his mind.

"Ships in bottles..." he started.

"They make up the body of the model trains, you see," I explained to Mom. "I'm learning how to reduce the resonant vibrations by altering the track gauge so the bottles don't chip or crack."

"Indeed," said Dad.

Genius stuff, thought Mom, then she said, "I lost my job today. No severance package." She tried another smile. "I hope these shipping trains in bottles aren't too expensive."

"They're not, dear."

"I got a grant from the Department of Defense!" I said. They laughed at that, Dad a little too hard.

I slipped down to the basement to let my parents have their fight about money in peace.

I was getting pretty bored with the dump and a rat almost bit Daniel, so we stopped going. Dad continued to leave early in the day, leaving me with Geri, who started vacuuming the carpets a lot. I mean she did it every day. She called me downstairs to move the furniture and everything. Daniel got me a reprieve one day by taking me with him to the UPS building. I waited by the loading dock with him.

"What are we waiting for? Did you buy a bunch of smoke detectors?" I asked him so he wouldn't know I knew that he bought commercial grade uranium online.

"No, I bought commercial grade uranium online. Perfectly legal." About ten minutes later, he signed for his uranium and put the box in the trunk of his car. Then we drove to the FedEx shipping center a few blocks away. There he answered to "Jerry Wallace," Mom's maiden name, and quickly flashed her old passport that he had put his picture on and then re-laminated to claim another box. That one went on my lap for the drive home. I wasn't too happy about that because it was heavy and radioactive. Since the sample was only twenty percent Uranium-235 I didn't have to be that worried, but you know, testicles.

He parked the car a block from the house and we cut through the Pasalquas' so that we ended up on the side of the house. I squirmed through the basement window Daniel left open, then dropped down the floor. Daniel walked the block back to get the first box, which I placed against the western wall, and then the second box, which I put against the opposite wall. Our Americium-241 loads were north and south, of course. Upstairs, Geri was watching one of those shows where your neighbor paints your living room orange.

Once we had the uranium, we were back in business. I pretended to join the chess club so that Daniel and I could drive around to get the rest of our supplies. Ever since the ferry across the sound to Bridgetown exploded thanks to sabotage, downtown Port Jameson was really suffering economically, so it was easy to buy some hydrofluoric acid from the glass etching guy, except that he was napping when we came by so we had to bang on the doors till he woke up. We poured it over our samples to make uranium tetrafluoride. I'm not a genius or anything, I'm just telling you what Dad was thinking. He got the recipe out of some old hippie magazine called *Seven Days*, and his schooling took care of the details.

Anyway, getting to uranium tetrafluoride was the easy part. The basement's ventilation was too poor to handle the fluorine gas we would need to create uranium hexafluoride, and once we got that we still had to separate the U-235 we needed from the junk U-238. The hippie magazine was no help there. It said: "Fill a standard-size bucket one-quarter full of liquid uranium hexafluoride. Attach a six-foot rope to the bucket handle. Now swing the rope (and attached bucket) around your head as fast as possible. Keep this up for about forty-five minutes. Slow down gradually, and very gently put the bucket on the floor." That's funny because except for this one thing, the article wasn't a joke.

Dad thought he could sneak into his old job, but security was tightened after the tuition riots, and all his old cronies had also been laid off and escorted from campus. They didn't even get to pack up their stuff—their little toys and family photos were mailed to them afterwards. Our uranium tetrafluoride wasn't exactly improving with age either. The next morning, Geri was at her networking club downtown. Dad checked me for hair loss and melanoma, made me some eggs, and then left in the car. Two hours later he came back home on foot and with shoes full of smelly hundred dollar bills. In the basement, Dad handed me a copper pipe and told me to smack him in the head with it, hard, but not too hard, a few times.

"And watch the teeth, Lovebug."

So I did.

Dad gave me the credit card and had me buy a centrifuge on eBay from my computer while he lay on the couch and told Mom some story about two big black guys carjacking him.

We bubbled the fluorine gas into our uranium tetrafluoride to get uranium hexafluoride and for safety's sake did it in the pool shed. Then all we had to do was get a jar of calcium pills from the vitamin store in the mall, crush them to powder, and add it to the uranium hexafluoride. The reaction was pretty neat; it sizzled and smelled like a playground jungle gym. Then we had calcium fluoride, which just looks like salt, and flakes of U-235. We separated that with a colander, and just used hammers to smash the U-235 filings together. Dad did half, then he sent me with the rest of the gunk to the basement to hammer together my U-235 mass.

Are you getting all this? I'm sorry if you're bored, but building your own nuclear bomb may be important for your future later. We're almost at the good part.

Daniel dug the old garden gnome out of the garage and used a blowtorch to open it at the seams. He cut open a tennis ball and put the two sub-critical masses of Americium-241 on opposite ends of it, sticking them to the inside of the ball with rubber cement. That went into the gnome's head. One of the two sub-critical masses of U-235 went right below it and the other into the gnome's base. Then he took apart one of my remote control cars (the cool Sidewinder Neon that does wheelies and 360s, if you're into radio control). One of the servos and the battery box were wedged into the gnome too. All Dad had to do was press a button on the controller. The tennis ball would be squeezed together, making the Americium go critical. That would send the U-235 mass in the head crashing through all the Styrofoam noodles we packed into the body of the gnome and into the U-235 mass in the base, and then that would go critical too, setting off a one megaton explosion.

"Dad, maybe we should take the batteries out of the radio control," I said.

He nodded. "Yeah..." he said, slowly, "but you can never find triple-As when you need them."

"I'll hang on to them for you."

"Okay, Herb. Don't misplace them."

Once we put the gnome back on the lawn and achieved neighborhood nuclear superiority, there were only two things left to do.

Tell the world, and declare independence.

And tell Mom.

2

We had to tell Geri first because her laptop was the only one with an anony-fax/modem. She used to like to send cranky faxes to different companies about there not being enough filling in a Pop-Tart or whatever, to get coupons for free stuff. We had a lot of faxes to send too. Daniel paced the house, trying to decide what to tell her first. *Hi Geri. I love you. That's why I want to send peace treaties to all the members of the Brotherhood of Evil Nations. Also, I built a nuclear bomb and possibly irradiated Herbert.* Or would the bomb news be a better lead? *Honey, you know I only want what's best for you and Herbie, and in this topsy-turvy world, I really feel that we need a one-megaton nuclear weapon. It's not even half a Hiroshima. Don't worry about breaking the law, we're our own country now. And a nuclear power to boot!*

When Mom came home from running her last errands as an American, Dad quickly made his decision. "Hi Geri," he said, then kissed her on the cheek. "Borrowing your laptop. Need to fax some resumes. C'mon, Herb, help your old man with something for a change."

I had a whole bunch of ideas for what to call our new country—Nuketown, Gnomeville, New America—but Dad just said "Weinbergia" and that was that. So much for democracy, I guess, but I didn't get to name the United States either. He wrote up a quick one-page treaty, offering peace and free trade to any signatory. Then we started faxing, thanks to numbers we found on different government web-sites or *The CIA World Factbook*. We did ten numbers at once, and with only 140 other countries, we were done in no time. Of course, most of the foreign countries were in different time zones, so who knows how many faxes our treaty would be buried under in the morning? Maybe some Mongolian janitor would think we were joking, sign the treaty on behalf of The People's Republic Of The Second Floor Utility Closet, and start his own national movement by mistake.

Or on purpose. Like you.

"Okay, now we'll…" Daniel said.

"Tell Ge…uh, Mom?" It's hard to call my parents Mom and Dad sometimes. I hear them thinking of themselves, and one another, by their real names all the time.

"Yes." Then he blinked the thought away, still afraid of Geri. "No, we need a press release first!" Dad posed, hands over the keyboard, ready to create his very own Declaration of Independence. "Herbie, you think we should mention the A-bomb?"

"Mmm, not yet," I said. I was worried about snipers.

It was easy enough to find email addresses and fax numbers to the only TV station near Port Jameson, the one that had nightly news in between all the *M*A*S*H* and *Seinfeld* reruns. Port Jameson doesn't have a daily paper, but it does have a weekly, *The Herald-Times-Beacon*. My picture was in it last year when I won the Brainstormers Academic Bowl trophy for the district. I could have gone to State up in Albany too, but I get sick on long bus rides, so I dropped a few questions about physics, ironically enough. Looked like my picture was going to be in the paper again.

Daniel wrote up the press release, and recited it in a loud and goofy "Greetings And Salutations" voice as he composed. "I, High King Daniel the First of Weinbergia, do hereby claim the property that was once known as 22 Hallock Road as my demesne and grange, free and independent from all law or governmental incursions of the United States of America..." It was funny, like an old cartoon. So I decided not to tell him that Mom had come home and was downstairs listening to his voice booming through the drop ceiling.

King Daniel continued, "And the brave people of Weinbergia, in the spirit of peace and the brotherhood of all men and women, propose to offer the olive branch of peace to the many and varied warring nations. Let our example guide you all in a quest for understanding and human rights. But be aware, the Kingdom and Realm is prepared to defend itself against interlopers and enemies external and in..."

"What the hell are you doing, Dan?" It was Mom, in the doorway, bemused. Dad didn't quite know what to say. He wanted to call her his beautiful Queen and make it seem like a joke so she would laugh and all would be back to normal.

Daniel wasn't even sure why we had built that bomb after all, except to make him feel that he was in control of things. That under his roof, he had some power.

Dad smiled. "Remember how we used to be, back in college? Protesting apartheid, living with Crazy Rob in the vegan house?"

Geri just raised an eyebrow. "You're not...writing our Congressman, are you? They'll send the FBI here for sure.

You can't fool around like that anymore, not since the wars,"
she said, more annoyed than worried.

Dad quickly hit the return key, and stood up. "Oh no,
nothing like that. Let's have lunch."

The FBI was at the Weinbergian border by the time I was eating my post-lunch ice cream sandwich. They didn't invade. It
was a recon mission, two agents. They asked the Pasalaquas if
Daniel was nuts. The Cases they asked if Daniel was an alco-
holic, recently divorced, or "one of those hippie types." An
agent asked the Levines if Daniel had ever said anything anti-
Semitic. Tanya, the wife, asked, "Anti-Semitic? Like what?"
The agent suggested, "Well, something like 'I hate the Jews'
or 'You're a dirty Jew' perhaps?" Tanya just shut the door on
him.

The feds left after taking a peek at the catalogs Geri left
behind in the mailbox, and parked a few blocks away. When
the coast was clear, our border station (the porch), was
besieged by foreign nationals.

"Yo Danny! You in there!" Joe Pasalaqua shouted through
the screen door. A few feet away Nick Levine parted the top
of the bushes obscuring the dining room window and peered
in. "I don't see anyone. Are they home?"

"The car's here," Tommy Case pointed out. He was on our
lawn, right by our little garden gnome NORAD, actually.
"They must be home." Nobody in Port Jameson walks anywhere, it's true. "Let's just call."

"What if the lines are tapped, Tommy?" Nick asked.

"What if the feds have a parabolic antenna pointed at us
from three blocks away?" Tommy said.

"Hey, Dan-NEEEE!" Joe called out.

My father was in the bathroom. Geri opened the door but kept the screen door closed because she didn't like Joe because he was a garbage man.

"Hello?"

"The FBI just came to my house to ask about your husband."

"Ohmigod," Mom said like it was one word, then quickly shut the door. The three men laughed as the shriek of "Daaaaaan!" went up inside the house.

I was in my room upstairs, reading comic books and minds.

Dad was finally ready, after almost puking. He smoothed his shirt with his palms, slipped the radio control into his pocket and walked across the dining room and kitchen, smiling at Geri rather than answering her, then headed out onto the lawn to shoo the interlopers off of our ancestral lands.

"Howdy boys," Dan said, arms held out wide, the radio control looking conspicuously suspicious (that almost rhymes, I like that) in his right hand. "I'm going to need to ask you to get off my lawn and step to the curb."

The men did so, walking backwards to keep from turning their back on Dad. Tommy Case was really worried, Joe Pasalaqua had already decided that he could do one of his old wrestling moves on Dad and take him out if he had to, and Nick Levine was wondering if somehow LSD was involved, and if he should just go back home before something bad happened.

"If you would like to enter the Kingdom of Weinbergia,

I'm afraid you'll have to apply for a visa first. You can fax an application," said my dad. Then he laughed.

"Oh Lord, you're insane!" That was Levine.

Tommy Case nodded toward the remote, "What do you have there, Daniel?"

"This is my Department of Defense. I don't mind telling it's a trigger for a one-megaton nuclear weapon."

"Bullcrap," Joe said.

"Is there anyone we can call for you, Daniel? Do you have a doctor? Has your health insurance lapsed?" Nick said.

"That looks a lot like a toy, Dan." That was Tommy.

"It's home brew, yes, but I don't need much."

"C'mon, whole countries can't build nukes, Danny!" said Joe.

"Sure they can," Daniel said, "it's that they can't build nuclear weapons powerful enough to compete with US standard. And they can't create an intercontinental delivery system. Weinbergia needs neither."

"I do not believe there is a nuclear weapon anywhere near here," said Nick.

"Eh, there's probably one on the submarine under the Long Island Sound," said Joe, then he laughed his little fake tough guy *heh-heh-heh*.

"Why would you start your own country? Why arm yourself? Are you in a militia? I mean, you have such a nice house, a smart son. I know you've been having some financial problems…" asked Nick, casting a glance at the beat-up old station wagon.

Dad's eyes widened. "Why? Why won't you declare independence! This country is going down the tubes. We're fighting forty wars with forty countries for no reason."

"Now that is not true," said Tommy sharply, "we need to protect ourselves from outside threats."

"Well, so do I."

"That is not the same. Look at Canada, they could attack us at any moment. They're all perched on the border. They don't think like we do. They're jealous."

"And Syria," said Nick. "Those people are all insane. Mexico too. Didn't Mexico threaten to cut off their oil pipeline?"

"That was *after* we started funding the New Villa Army."

"We have every right to make sure our friends are secure," Nick said.

"Shaddup, shaddup," said Joe. "I don't like the wars either, but c'mon Danny, you don't have a bomb, and if you do, someone's just gonna shoot you in your sleep." With that Joe stepped back onto the lawn, and Nick and Tommy followed.

"I'm sure you're upsetting Geri, Dan," said Nick.

"And think of Herbert," said Tommy.

"Back off!" Dad said, pointing his remote at them. "What is it about you Americans? You threaten me every day with your wars and weaponry, but can't stand the fact that anyone else in this world shows a little independence."

"Don't you badmouth America, Daniel. We have men overseas, fighting for your freedoms!" Nick said, his anger rising. "You know, I noticed you didn't fly the flag on the Fourth this year."

"Or on Flag Day!" said Tommy.

"Are you being paid off by the Mexicans?" Nick asked.

"I bet it's Brazil! Didn't you go to Brazil," said Tommy, raising his arms and twitching his fingers in the quote-mark gesture, "*on vacation* last year?"

"That was Barbados, Tom."

"Barbados recently refused a request to use their airspace, you know," Nick said.

"Given what happened to the last few countries to let us use their airspace, I could see why," Daniel said.

"Given what happened to the last few countries that refused, Daniel, you'd think they'd be happy to allow our men to fly safely over their skies," Nick said. "Unless they had some sort of agent planning nuclear blackmail!"

"My God, you're a traitor!" Tommy declared. "Let's get that remote away from him right now!"

Both Tommy and Nick turned to Joe, hoping he'd be the one to attack Dad. He just shrugged.

"Listen. I've seen the garbage you people throw away," Joe said. He was coming to his own political conclusion even as he was speaking. "It's disgusting, a waste. Whole families can live out of one of your garbage cans, Tommy, and you know what, since the wars started after 9/11, they have been. I don't care about foreign policy. I just want everyone to leave everyone else alone. But if you really built a bomb, Danny…that's messed up. What are you gonna do anyway, set it off if someone steps on your grass?" He shrugged big.

"I'm going to go home," Tommy said, "and I'm going to get my gun. You hear me Daniel? I own a gun!"

Daniel shrugged big this time. Nick sneered as Tommy strode off. "This isn't a joke, traitor. You're in a boatload of trouble…" He stopped as the news van for TV-66, the local station, turned the corner and idled by the Western front. Its transmission pole, with its dish top, was as high as the window I was watching my dad from. Dad felt a rush of excitement; he had a bit of a crush on Deborah Stanley-Katz, one of TV-66's news anchors. They sent her out for the biggest stories, like medical waste washing up on the beach, or sad black people who had their welfare taken away. One time she interviewed the governor, and Dad liked the way her blazer would go down to her waist, all snug and...

Out popped Rich Pazzaro, the fat weatherman who also did the stories about pie-eating contests and the circus coming to town. Inside the van, a bored-looking cameraman was leisurely getting his rig together. This was not going to be a big deal tonight.

"How-deeeee!" Rich said, doing his weather shtick. He said "How-deeee!" to things like hurricanes and chimpanzees on TV. "Which one of you is the king of Weintraubia?"

Joe laughed and hiked his thumb at Dad. "Right here, here's your Lordship."

Daniel smiled as Rich crossed the border and entered our country. "I'm Daniel, I'm the King of Wein*bergia*." He offered his left hand to Rich, who juggled his microphone to shake. "Welcome to my homeland." At that moment, Tommy's long stride took him to our border. He had a pistol and leveled it at Dad sideways. "Die, traitor!" Dad pulled hard on Rich's hand and dragged the fat guy in front of him.

"Stay back, I have a human shield!" Dad declared, wrapping the arm holding the radio control around Rich's neck. Rich, suddenly frantic, waved with his free hand for his cameraman, but when the guy came rushing out without the camera, Rich waved him back on the car.

"Rich Pazzaro!" said Tommy. "My wife loves you!" He kept the gun pointed at Dad, or really at Rich's chest. The bullet would go right through it, probably, he figured.

"Uhm…listen," Rich said. Dad wasn't choking him, but he was a little short of breath from being in the hold. "I just want…an interview." The camera operator crossed the border and shouldered his camera. "If that gun's loaded," Rich said, "we can go live."

Rich and Dad both looked at Tommy hopefully. Tommy nodded.

"Okay," said the cameraman, "we've got to wait a minute for the clearance, but the truck is already patched through."

"Can I get…a little…background…on you, Your Highness?"

"You can call me Daniel, Mr. Pazzaro."

"He's a traitor, what else do you need to know?" Tommy asked.

"Why don't you lower the gun?" Nick asked.

"Why don't you just leave if you don't want to be on television?" Tommy asked back. "Right Joe…" he turned to look at Joe, who had already turned around and was halfway home.

"Live in ten, Rich," the cameraman said.

"Married?"

"Yes, my wife loves you, remember?"

"Yes, I'm married," Daniel said.

"Oh no you are not!" It was Mom. She had been watching from the kitchen, afraid to go outside. Now she was going to defect.

"Four...three..." then the cameraman counted "two...one" silently.

"We're here...live...hostage situation. There is a gun pointed at me by..."

Tommy leaned in to address the mic, and stared into the camera. "Thomas Case, proud American."

"And I...am in the clutches...of?" Rich said, trying to bend his arm so that Dad could talk into the microphone.

"You are the guest of King Daniel The First of Weinbergia."

Mom rushed by in the background of the shot. Rich called out to her, "Ma'am...you are—"

"Leaving!" she said, getting into the car. She slammed the door hard, and peeled out of the driveway, kicking gravel into America. She wasn't even thinking of me as she pulled on to Hallock and drove off. The cameraman panned right to get a shot of the car.

"Ahem, proud American here!" said Tommy, and the camera panned back.

Rich, his face reddening, pointed the mic at Nick. "Who are you...with?"

Nick nodded toward Tommy, "I'm with him..." then he looked at the gun, which Tommy was having a hard time holding steady. "Uhm...I mean, no. I'm with America! You know, I support the President." He nervously turned on his heel and not knowing what else to do, saluted the camera in case the President was watching.

"Let me explain," said Daniel, loosening his grip on Rich just a bit. Rich obliged by pulling the mic back towards him. "I have constructed a nuclear weapon using legal materials

found on the Internet. I have declared my independence from
the United States of America and have sent peace treaties to
all nations that the US is currently at war with, occupying, or
bound to by treaty agreements. I want peace and freedom for
myself and my nation. I also open my borders to anyone else
interested in ending these horrible wars and leading a life
where we don't have to be afraid of losing our jobs, or of saying the wrong thing and being interrogated, and where our
kids won't grow up to be drafted. However, I do not rule out
the use of nuclear weapons in achieving our aims of peace.
Thank you very much. Press conference over!" With that Dad
yanked hard and pulled Rich off his feet, and dragged him
back into the house. Rich, always the professional, shouted
into the mic, "This has been a live report for TV-66! Rich
Pazzaro, saying for perhaps the last time, how-deeeeeee!"
The mic cord stretched to its limit at the porch, and Rich let
it go.

The camera turned back to Tommy and Nick, who were
standing around like a pair of simpletons. "Should I shoot?"
Tommy asked. Nick shrugged, looked into the camera and
said, "God Bless America? Can we get some help? Police?
Homeland Security?" The shot faded to black.

Dad made a racket, pushing the door open with his butt and
dragging an uncooperative Rich inside with him. "Herbie!"
he called out, "Time for lunch! And set a third plate." I came
downstairs as he let go of Rich to let him catch his breath.

"What are you going to do to me?"

Dad shrugged. "Well, you can be a reporter or a prisoner
of war. Either way, you're getting pizza."

I walked into the room. "Hello?"

"Hi son, meet Rich Pazzaro, from TV."

"Hi."

Rich looked me over, recognizing me. "Brainstormers?"

I nodded. "Yeah." Then to Dad, "Can we eat now?"

"Absolutely." Dad went to the fridge. The little interior light went on as always, then cut out, along with all the other lights and digital clocks, and the air conditioning.

"They cut the power."

"This means war."

In the distance, sirens and mad thoughts converged upon us.

It was dark except for the occasional helicopter spotlight or flashing red siren. The police had come first, only to be replaced by the FBI, who were in turn replaced by some guys from the local National Guard and big men from Homeland Security. They had an especially sensitive Geiger counter out there, so knew we weren't kidding about having the bomb. That's why we were still alive. The three of us sat on the floor so that we couldn't be seen through the windows, and munched on cold pizza. During the brief interludes of silence within all the barked orders, helicopter rotor noises, and hut-hut-huts of soldiers taking up positions on our borders, Rich asked us questions.

"So, was this all part of your plan?" he asked Daniel. Rich was expecting Dad to go nuts and end this with some sort of murder-suicide thing.

Daniel shrugged. "Once we're established as a country, we'll have trading partners, we'll be able to live independently."

"But that's not going to happen!" Rich was getting agitat-ed again. His mind was like a wave on the beach. He'd get mad, break up, then collect himself slowly and calmly, only to make another crazed rush for the jetty. "Nobody supports you. You have no idea what CNN, hell, what Fox News, is doing to you! All anyone knows about you is that you have a dirty bomb and that you kidnapped a beloved local weather-man."

"If you'd like to leave, you can," I said. "They won't shoot you. They haven't demanded you be returned yet because they're hoping you'd be able to talk some sense into us."

"How do you know that?"

"I'm a genius," I lied.

"Does anyone want a drink?" Daniel said. "I have some wine, if you want, Mr. Pazzaro?"

"Sure."

"Coke for me."

"It'll be warm, son."

"That's fine."

Dad crawled into the kitchen. Rich leaned in and whis-pered, "Why are you so calm? Doesn't this frighten you? Don't you think your dad is crazy?"

I shrugged. "Not any crazier than the President." And this is true. I know. I checked.

"We're going to die here."

"No, we're not."

Dad came back, duck-walking and spilling some of my soda. We drank out of our plastic picnic cups silently. The hel-icopters were making another pass, and would have drowned us out anyway.

Sitting on a floor is a great way to conserve energy, and being surrounded by army guys really gets the adrenaline running. So at 3 AM, Dad and I were awake. Dad was starting to get nervous. Would we live to see the sun? Were the other countries even aware of us? Did they even care? Rich was slumped in a corner, sometimes snoring, sometimes waking with a start to ask Dad when he was going to surrender to the inevitable, sometimes to ask me if there was any pizza left. There wasn't, but I made him a peanut butter sandwich with Geri's seven-grain bread. He seemed to like that.

"We should check the email, Dad."

"How?" Rich murmured. He was half-asleep. "No power."

"Mom's laptop has a battery."

"Damn, you're right!" Dad crawled off on his belly. Outside, they started serenading us with very loud banjo music, to try to break our will.

Dad was back in a minute, crawling to us lopsided, with the laptop tucked under one arm. He opened it up and we all gathered around to take in the white glow of the screen. It was good to be around electricity again. The feds had kept the phone on because they wanted to call us tomorrow, and they wanted to see if we would call some terrorists, or grandma, or somebody like that. We used the old dial-up account and checked our email.

Seventy-three new messages. Cheap mortgages, porn, porn, porn (Dad wished I'd turn away, but I didn't. I was a prince now, after all). A few folks had seen us on TV and sent us messages, most of them wishing us dead. Porn, porn, enlarge your breasts, free fake college degrees, and Palau.

The Olbiil Era Kelulau, the Senate of the tiny Pacific island of Palau, had agreed to sign the treaty. We were at peace with them. Tomorrow, they'd appeal to the UN on our behalf. Palau was with us, and wanted to open trade talks. They had pearls, coconuts. What did we have, they wanted to know?

We had the bomb. If anyone messed with Palau, we'd destroy Port Jameson. And we had me. There wasn't a secret in the world I couldn't dig out of someone's brain.

Palau is a sunny land full of friendly, cheerful people. In this it is like every other country in the world, except Weinbergia. It's true. Cold, bitter Russians are friendly and cheerful. Terror cells are friendly and cheerful, not as they plot away in dank basements, but when they are with their families and friends, or eating good local food. Women covered head to toe in those nasty veils—the ones who get stoned to death or shot if they go outside with their face showing—they are friendly and cheerful when they're inside or down by a water-hole with the other women, where no men can see. The men who throw the rocks are friendly and cheerful too, even if they're doing it because all their friends are, or because there is a gun to their own backs.

People all over the world are exactly the same. Cheerful and friendly and deathly afraid to act that way because some-one will shoot them if they do, so they turn on each other like two dogs at the park. That's what happened on Palau. There's a military base there, American. That's half the reason Palau is its own country instead of just part of Micronesia. I won-der if having Palau would push Micronesia over into being

Mininesia. Anyway, the soldiers at the base, friendly and cheerful though they are, like to have sex with local women. When the women get pregnant, the soldiers just hide behind their guns and fences. There are lots of soldiers' babies in Palau, and not a lot of money for them.

The old people, friendly and cheerful and thankful for their grandchildren, have been waiting for a moment for a long time, nearly a generation. When the founding of Weinbergia hit the news, they went out under cover of night to find their elected officials. It's a small country, only 20,000 people or so; the whole government has fewer than 40 people, and they live pretty much like anyone else, except they wear Italian suits with American labels. The old people came to them with gifts of fruit and finely-weaved baskets. Then after a nice meal and sweet dessert, out came the machetes. For the first time ever, Palau's government did something the United States didn't like. Behind the worried debate that morning, even the members of the Olbiil Era Kelulau were secretly friendly and cheerful as they voted to save us. People are cheerful and friendly everywhere. Even here in fabled Weinbergia, where Rich really got into the swing of things with Dad.

The power was back on. Not because of Palau, but because the news media was out in force. Their power generators were too noisy for local ordinance (Tommy Case complained), so the feds turned our juice back on and let the TV cameras tie into our power. The meter was spinning like crazy. *Just one more form of brutal American oppression*, thought Dad, but he was happy and cheerful. We had water too, and they didn't cut our cable either, so we could watch our own house. Rich hogged the webcam all morning and happily detailed the moment-by-moment "hostage drama" that was taking place. He covered the camera lens with the fat palm of his hand when I walked in with some toaster waffles—they were the kind he especially liked, blueberry and bacon bits— but then dug into breakfast with his fists wrapped around the fork and butter knife. It was gripping web-television, for sure, and after that the major news networks stopped calling Rich a hostage and suggested that he had been won over by our relentless propaganda, or maybe drugs in the waffles.

Rich did come around pretty quickly. By noon he was spread all over the couch and taking calls from around the world from the cell phone one of the Army guys had slipped in through the mail slot.

"Your Highness!" he called out.

"Yeah…" I said. He had been asking me stupid questions all morning.

"I meant your Dad, Sport!"

I hate being called Sport or Kiddo or any of those stupid names. Ace. Ace would have been cool. But you have to shoot down a plane or something to be called Ace. I resolved at that moment to start working on it.

From the basement, my father's hollow voice asked what was up.

"It's Hollywood, baby! Want to sell the rights to this?"

"It'll have to be a US/Weinbergian co-production," Daniel shouted.

"I'll see!" Rich shouted back, then more quietly into the phone he explained our demands. He paused, smiling like he was still on TV. Then, "Hello? Hello? How-deee?" He frowned. "Damn. Hey Ace…"

Much better. "Yeah?"

"Care for an interview?"

"Sure." I walked over to the couch while Rich picked himself up and diddled with the laptop's webcam in an attempt to get a shot that didn't make him look like a lazy slug. I stood by, wearing a TV commercial kid smile until my cheeks started hurting. Finally, after licking his fingers and running them through his hair (yes, gross), Rich was ready for his remote.

"Rich Pazzaro, embedded in what a small, dangerous family has decided to call Weinbergia," he said in a serious whisper to the world on the other side of the lens. "Day three of America's nuclear crisis. I'm here with young Herbert. His father calls him 'prince' but to his mother, and America, he is a hostage. A human shield." I rolled my eyes.

He leaned back, wrapped an arm around me and brought me closer to the camera for an intimate shot, then asked, "Do you feel that you're in danger here?"

"Duh!" I said. Then I grabbed the little webcam and twisted it so it pointed out the window. On the laptop screen, I could see a huddle of American soldiers gathered around a TV monitor. They looked up toward the camera when they saw themselves on TV and waved to me and the world.

Rich took the cam back and turned it back around for a close-up of himself. "He's a boy who loves his father. That family tie, exploited in a game of nuclear brinksmanship." He turned to me again, "What are your days like here, under siege. Do you miss your school friends?"

"Well, most of them are upstate at computer camp anyway.

I think I'm learning more here. I'm also in charge of a lot of stuff. Did you know that the national bird of Weinbergia is the bluebird? I declared it so this morning," I said. Nobody is going to shoot a kid who says he likes bluebirds. It's true. I double-checked the brains of everyone outside on the front lines before picking the bird.

"Aaaand," I said, nudging Rich out of the way and sticking my head right up to the camera so I'd look all cute and distorted—you know, the way you look reflected in a doorknob or something, "I'm working on our official language, Weinbergian. For example, if I wanted to say, 'Hi, my name is Prince Herbert The First,' I'd say, 'Lo, yo soy nameo izzo Fresh Herbie Primo.' Pretty cool, huh?" I smiled wide for the camera. I'm not a hunk or anything, but I could feel, all over your country, little girls deciding to start fansites about me. A million LiveJournal entries were born.

Fun Facts About Weinbergia

Name: Weinbergia

Telephone area code: 631

Area: 2000 sq. ft. 2 1/2 baths

Land boundaries: United States of America, specifically the Pasalqua and Case residences

Terrain: Parquet floors

Highest mountain: The tip of Rich Pazzaro's ego

Natural resources: Uranium. Fear. Hope.

Population: 3ish

Population density: 1/ 666 sq. ft

Distribution: 100% suburban

Life expectancy: We're trying not to think about that

Capital: King Daniel's not above calling the master bath "the throne room," unfortunately

Flag: Take the McDonald's golden arches on a red background, and turn it upside down so it looks like a W

Government: "As long as you're under my roof, you'll do what I say!"—King Daniel I.

National anthem: "In The Garden Of Freedom" (sung to the tune of "In A Gadda-Da-Vida")

Languages: English

Currency: Dollar

Climate: Central air

Religion: Vague liberal agnosticism. Judaism. Known to say "Jesus Christ!" at stupid stuff on TV.

Exports: Punditry, fodder

That afternoon, I was nearly lulled to sleep by the clockwork thinking of the first line of soldiers as they turned first to the right, then to the left, rifles high and Dad in their sights as he mowed the lawn on the northern frontier of Weinbergia. The landscapers Mom had hired decided not to come in today and given the politico-legal difficulties we found ourselves in, Dad didn't want to give the US any more ammunition by getting the Terrytown Fire District all mad, too. That's what he said anyway, but deep down he just wanted to test American mettle, and get a little time off from Rich.

So he mowed the lawn, slowly and carefully, back and forth, while forty-five GIs trained their guns on him. At the end of the block, Operations buzzed with contingencies and possibilities. Should we shoot Dan Weinberg and rush the

place? Does he have some sort of spoilsport option in place
that would set off the bomb if his heart stopped? Is it biomet-
rical? How could it be; the guy's out there in a tank top, white
shorts, and sandals with socks? Maybe the kid? What about
the kid, what about the children?

What about me? I was scraping the black stuff off of a
grilled cheese Rich had tried to make for himself. "Here ya go
Herb," he had said as he knocked on my already-open door
and offered me the sandwich, "you're probably hungry, so I
thought I'd fix you something."

I hate it when people "fix" food, don't you? Especially
when it was as broken as this second-hand sandwich. But I
was hungry and it gave me something to do other than fall
asleep listening to the droning thoughts of the soldiers outside. That's when the shooting happened. It went like this, in
the head of PFC Frank Torres, who's from Brentacre, just a
few miles from Port Jameson:

Left Left Left Left
Right Right Right Right
Left Left Left Left
Right Right Right Turn onto 347
Left Left Left at the mall
Right Home Where I Started From
Left Left Home At Eighteen
Right Right Back Here
So Close Target Is So Close
Miss Miss Mami Mami
Miss Miss Don't Miss Target

Then he fired by mistake—a psychic twitch of homesickness and boredom—but missed. My father dropped to the ground, leaving the lawn mower to lurch forward and roll a bit. A couple of slugs tore through it too before a squad leader bellowed, "HOLD YOUR FIRE!" The guns stopped, so did the fiery anxiety and whooping joy of the line. Everyone lowered their rifles, vainly hoping that the captain would blame the other guy.

My father hopped back to his feet and fists curled, marched to the border, nearly smacking into the equally red-faced captain who was up from his lawn chair and ready to scream till his men crapped themselves. They met at right angles and stared, both wide-eyed and huffing like bulls.

My father spoke first. "Can't a man cut the grass in peace?" he demanded, and really, that's all he was thinking. The captain was nonplussed, so Dad turned to the line of troops. "Who shot at me? Which one of you Yankee imperialists shot at me?" He pointed randomly at a guilty looking soldier. "Was it you?"

"Hey man, I just shot your mower," he said, defeated. A few heads down, Torres mentally snickered. The captain, Whiting, felt his control of the situation, illusory as it was, slipping away from him, and stepped in the path of my father's pointed finger.

"Mister Weinberg," he started.

"Mister President."

"President Weinberg, please. This could spiral into an…incident."

"An international incident! Perhaps even an occurrence. Where's the media now, when you need them? You're all blocking the curb, how am I supposed to use my trimmer later?" my father demanded of nobody in particular.

The squad captain put a hand on Dad's shoulder and said. "I understand. I have a lawn too. Back home." Then he nodded in that way men nod when they want other men to nod back at them. And Dad did. Then both of them looked toward the lawn mower, which just sat there and smoked through its new bullet holes, uselessly.

Dad was back inside for the afternoon, giving his side of the story to Rich and the webcam, while outside, a couple of grunts finished the job with a John Deere helicoptered in from the nearest Home Depot and a pair of hand-clippers. They did it checkerboard-style, going over the lawn twice, except for a couple of feet around the garden gnome.

Overnight, Dad became the hero to billions—he'd stared down the American war machine, brought them to heel, and made them do chores. Captain Whiting was relieved of command overnight and is currently in the brig somewhere, staring in front of a mirror, trying to pee. Almost exactly like me.

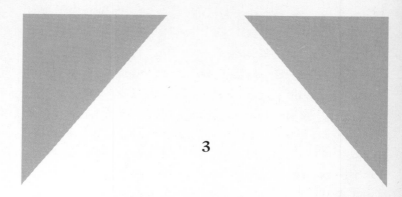

3

You think you know what happened. It was all over the news. My mother Geri sobbing into the cameras, the cult, the fist-fights in the United Nations, the daring raid, Rich's bravery...or was it treachery, blah blah blah. But you don't know what happened. What happened is that seven men and four women were at our door the next afternoon, all with pizzas. Rich and Daniel peered at the bunch nervously, with Rich trying to pull off the impossible trick of looking concerned enough to impress Dad and eager enough to impress the federal agents and army guys he was sure were behind the pizza deliveries.

Actually, all but two of the pizzas were sent by well-wishers who'd seen me chewing on an awful sandwich all night on the cam; the last two were fake deliveries by Adrienne and Kelly, two Port Jamesonites who wanted to come in from the cold. I helped them out by pointing at them through the screen door. "You and you can come in with the pizza, the rest of you...thanks but no thanks."

Nobody moved from the positions they had staked out, except for some pimple-faced kid who wobbled a bit, unsure of himself. Nobody listens to kids, you know. "Daaaad," I said.

"What, Herb? Why?"

I didn't need to think of anything clever as Adrienne just smiled widely and pushed the screen door open with her elbow. "How do you do?" she said, "How do you do?" She was older, like my mother, with a big Long Island mop of dyed black curls and bangs. Kelly slipped in right behind her and said "How are ya?" like a normal person. She was pretty normal, twenty-five, high hair, jingly earrings, that sort of thing. Dad closed both the screen and the main door, leaving the rest of the pizza delivery people with nothing else to do except make their way back to America with their pies and take their body-cavity searches like good citizens.

"There's no pizza in either of these," Rich said, annoyed. "Just…money."

"American?" Dad asked. Then he turned to the ladies. "That money's no good here."

Adrienne just smiled. "Every country has a store of American dollars. It's the least we could do. We're asylum seekers."

Kelly nodded. "You have to let us stay. It's crazy out there!" And they told their stories, mostly going on about how hard it was to make ends meet. They'd both been unemployed and met in the waiting room of a temp agency, then realized they were only ten miles from the border. Neither of them could find jeans in their size because the manufacturers found it cheaper to make clothing cut for people who didn't actually exist. American men were mean, and lazy in the bedroom. Kelly blushed and shot me an apologetic look as Adrienne explained that, but she was thinking about herself and Rich doing it in front of a weather map! And besides, they thought, they really wanted to be on TV. Ten minutes later I was in the basement, trying to figure out whether the old quilts Mom stored down there were machine washable, while Kelly raided the liquor cabinet and made cocktails for the adults.

Richard—he was calling himself Richard now, because he thought it sounded more presidential, or at least less friendly—interviewed a slightly tipsy Kelly later that night. She's one of those people who just get very sad when they drink, like there's a dark spring in her heart that just bubbles up to the surface whenever she forgets to pay attention.

"Sometimes," she said, looking down even though Rich reminded her three times to look at him (and four times to "try to look sexy") "—it's just, you know, hard. You go to work, stop to get some take-out on the way home, and watch other people live lives you can't on television. I don't even have anyone to shout at me in my living room, or to say funny things. You know?"

"Uhm. Sure." Rich ad-libbed. "Do you have a political agenda that you're hoping to carry out?"

"Well, I'm definitely against violence and nuclear proliferation. I guess I wanted to find some like-minded people."

"You came to the wrong place!" Dad shouted from the kitchen.

"He's right. Weinbergia is a nuclear power," Rich said.

"Yeah, but you guys aren't going to use it. I mean, it would be suicide."

"How's that any different," Dad shouted again, "from America?"

Kelly looked at Rich, confused. Rich just nodded, a content-free nod. Yes, I acknowledge your existence. That kind of thing. Kelly finally shrugged and said, "I guess I just trust King Daniel more than the President. He seems kinder, more honest. Like a normal person. He doesn't wear a tie just because he knows he's going to be on television. I like that."

"So is that why you came here, to Weinbergia?"

"Well, I always wanted to go abroad."

Kelly, with her cow eyes and hollow voice, wasn't what you'd call telegenic. She came off as brainwashed, but really, she was simply emerging from years of American brainwashing. Kelly was confused and anxious—she may not have to go to work every day anymore, just to have enough money to buy cute shoes and Healthy Choice entries, just so that she could find some guy who would smile and lift things for her between football games, just so she could have a kid who'd grow up proud to be an American just because that's where he plopped out of her. A kid who'd in turn do the same thing. This wasn't the tickertape parade and celebrity hugs freedom she was expecting. It was a dull, throbbing freedom; more like a headache.

"How do you feel about being this close to what some call a terrorist nuclear device?" Richard asked. "Are you afraid?"

"Not anymore than I was this morning. Forty wars on forty countries, that's us. That was me. Not now though. Terrorists are supposed to be everywhere. That's why they search your car on the Long Island Expressway, right?" She shrugged. "I mean, with everybody watching now, what are they gonna do, storm in and kill us? For what?"

"For having a nuclear device out on the lawn," Richard said. "Don't you think? Do you think that anyone should have the right to just threaten us with nukes?"

"No, I don't. I guess I really don't," Kelly said. "That's why I'm here." She and Richard stared at each other. He really wasn't a very good reporter, and Kelly mentally scratched him off her sex list. The interview was over and an awkward silence descended over all Weinbergia, except for the kitchen where Dad was trying to impress Adrienne by making an omelet. He was banging pots around like some ugly American.

All you probably saw of this on the news—unless you subscribed to the website anyway—was Kelly's dead eyes and her murmuring, "Well, I always wanted to go abroad." It's one of those dumb tricks the media use to make people they don't like look like morons, but they forgot that lots of people felt just like Kelly. With all the wars, and all the ruined diplomatic relationships, and with the five-hour long check-in lines at the airports, millions of people wanted to go abroad and couldn't. For a few of them, for almost of enough of *you* out there, you got the idea. Go abroad where it counts. Right up here.

Feel that, the tapping on your temple? That's me. Tap tap. Go abroad in your head, that's the message at least some people heard. That's what Kelly did, by emigrating to Weinbergia, and she wasn't the last. People, being generally happy, have a weird way of looking at the television or the Internet: they read something and decide that it secretly means something else, and they think that only they can see through the lies of the media. Their own opinions they've come to thanks to logic, or hard-earned experience, or Jesus showing up at the foot of their bed and telling them what time it is. Everyone else? Well, they're dupes and morons, emotional wrecks, or people who actually think *Jesus* showed up at the foot of their bed to tell them what time it is. And media people love this. Rich told me once, "As long as we get complaints from both the liberals and conservatives, we know that we're reporting the news right." That the media thinks it is telling the truth because everyone thinks they're lying—no matter what the news actually said and no matter what the audience originally thought—doesn't make much sense to me, but I checked a few heads over in the city and, geez, Rich was right.

So anyway, it was some vanishingly small percentage of the people who watched the interview, but they got the message: go abroad in your heads. Weinbergia's approval ratings plummeted, but the Great Haaj began. The next morning, the Long Island Expressway and Route 25A were choked with, well, Dad called them hippies. There were plenty of those: guys with long beards, ready smiles, and laid-back personalities. You know that movie where the rock band says of its amplifiers, "Well, these go to eleven"? These guys' emotions only went up to eight. There were women hippies too, mostly boiling under a happy surface (but happy again, under the boiling). Most people weren't hippies though: there were lots of nerds, some crazier than others. Tax cheats, college kids who made up their own languages in their spare time, a woman who called herself Doctress Arcologia who wanted to build a treehouse in the oak outside my window; in exchange she'd give us exclusive rights to market her perpetual motion machine: a generator hooked up to a motor.

Adrienne gave herself the job of border guard and decided to keep out anyone who she thought might want to sleep with or kill Dad. She mostly got it right too. Dad was a bit too busy to welcome his new subjects; one of the people who slipped past the border—he looked kind of like John Travolta, except fatter and dressed in unconvincing tie dye—handed my father a summons and then vanished back behind the line of American troops.

I had heard his thoughts coming, but I was too busy with Kelly to stop my Dad from taking the letter. Kelly had cornered me right outside of the upstairs bathroom.

"Hi there. I'm Kelly," she said.

"Hi. Herb."

She smiled, "Can I call you Prince Herbert?" Her mind was a dizzy array of anxieties and what she thought were Really Deep Thoughts (*Men are simple creatures, driven by appetites; women are driven by duty*) streaked with a low-level adrenaline rush. I liked her though, because she wasn't thinking what most adults do when they strike up a conversation with a kid. You know what I'm talking about, unless you're a kid. Then you probably just suspect it:

Aw look. The little person can talk. I wonder if it can say anything interesting if I ask it how old it is.

Hee hee, look at that little moron go!

But she didn't think that; she only thought, *I'm so lonely...and excited.* So of course I let her call me Prince Herbert. She tried a crooked curtsy, and I patted the air with my hand like a TV king might, because that's what she wanted me to do.

"Prince Herbert, can you tell me something?" she asked me. "What's the plan?"

"The plan?"

"Yes, I mean, what's next. You can't live in this house forever, not being part of America."

"Why not? People live in their houses all their lives and *are* part of America. And they do it without UN recognition."

Then she started up with that *moron* thinking. "You don't understand. I mean, you ever heard that saying 'No man is an island'? You can't just separate yourself from a country."

"Countries do it all the time. America did it in the first place."

"America had an army, kid. And it has a bigger one now. You just can't go challenging the world's largest superpower." So much for Prince Herbert.

"Well, that's what we're doing. Heck, that's what you're doing, Kelly. Why did you even emigrate?"

"I thought you'd have some answers!" She looked away from me and then out the window, brushing the curtain aside with her cheek to look at the swarm of weirdos snaking across the lawn, and the cordon of troops surrounding them. "I should have just stayed home."

"Well, what kind of answers were you expecting?" I knew the answer already, and also knew that she couldn't put it into words. The questions were there, though, like the flavored glop inside an unlabeled Valentine Day chocolate—even after you bite into it, you don't know what the hell you're eating. There were no answers for her; she wasn't even really looking for them. She just wanted to hear some set of words that would attack the glob and make it vanish, like antimatter.

"Well, you just seem so happy. How could you be happy knowing what will happen?"

Why was I so happy? I didn't really feel all that happy; never did. I mean it's not like I could move into my own apartment or anything. Even back when I kept a diary, I never wrote about being happy, except when recording what other people were thinking or experiencing, and they were generally happy about dumb stuff, like a football game or someone agreeing with them.

I guess I just liked the craziness of it all. That answer wasn't going to satisfy Kelly's brainglop so I did what I usually do at chess club. Kids aren't really very good chess players, except for the occasional supernerd, so it's no use reading their mind for the proper response to the moves —they don't know what the hell they're doing either. So what I'd do is poke around the mindscape of the club sponsor, or the guy in the next town who had all these chess books and who subscribed to all the chess magazines, and who always had three or four games going in his living room, and get the answer from him.

So I checked Dr. Phil and Dr. Laura and the social worker from school who asked me once why I never applied myself and The Pope and Billy Graham and Tom Hanks and all sorts of other people that make their living giving advice, or just being warm and giving their opinions, and came up with a response.

"Oh Kelly," I said, reaching out to touch her hand, "it'll all be all right."

"But—"

"It'll all work out for the best."

"They have so many gun—"

"Everything happens for a reason." I smiled a cereal commercial smile.

The glob in Kelly's brain melted and steamed out her ears, deflating her tension like a balloon. She leaned down and kissed me on the forehead. "You're right," she said. She was about to say something else but then turned to see as our new resident aliens marched up the steps by the dozen to use the upstairs restroom, full of pardon mes and I really gotta goes and ohmygod this isn't as big as I thought it would be on TVs and is this the right doors. "Herb-AY, my man!" one very very white guy said; he was in the lead and held out a palm for me to high-five.

I left him hanging.

Downstairs, Adrienne and Dad were frowning over the summons. In the corner, Rich was taping them. He had a new assistant, a teenager I recognized as a bagger from Pathmark—his job was apparently to take the lampshade off my mother's old lamp and hold it up behind the camera to make sure Dad squinted from the light, and that the rest of the room was cut up with stripes of shadow.

"Herbert, we have to talk," said Adrienne, whose brain was spinning with crazy thoughts of being my new mother. She saw herself in flickering black and white, wearing an apron and handing out bagged lunches to me and Rich, who in her little daydream was wearing dress shorts. Then out come the servants to drape a mink around her shoulders and place a tiara on her head. Weirdo.

"Your mother has filed a custody suit. Don't worry, your father is going to fight this all the way to the Supreme Court."

"No, I'm not," said Dad, "I'm going right to the General Assembly of the United Nations. This isn't a matter for family court, if they want Herb, they'll need to extradite him."

"Extradite me!" Okay, so it didn't mean what I thought it did at that very second. I checked Dad's mind for the actual meaning of the word, but really didn't feel all that much better.

"You're not going to go anywhere, Herbie, don't you worry," Adrienne said. I shot my Dad a look, and he shrugged. Then he announced, regally, "Nobody is going to leave Weinbergia against his or her will! We are a sovereign nation!"

"That's right!" shouted whoever was using the downstairs bathroom. A smattering of applause floated throughout the house like lost butterflies.

"Hear hear," said Adrienne, getting another stare from Dad. Then Rich stepped forward and pointed his camera at me. "Do you miss your mother?"

"Yes…, uh, I mean—" and that was that. I knew what he wanted to hear, *I knew it*, and it still just came flying out of my mouth anyway. I did miss her. Weinbergia was already filling up with hippies and morons (some lady with long gray hair and a tie-dyed skirt even got on her knees behind me to wave into the camera, I'm sure you saw it a million times on TV), the air outside stank of diesel fuel and ozone and I really just wanted things to be like they were before—when Dad and I were building the bomb. When we had time together and when my mother smiled to see us hanging out all the time.

So I said yes and the world heard it. There's a big difference between being able to know what's going to happen and being able to do something about it. I could feel them, the entire weight of the American military, the media, the factories, the great thinkers, all of them, arraying against Weinbergia. The first line of cordons were only scrubs—expendables—but beyond that the Special Operators lurked. They were holed up in the Red Berry Bed & Breakfast on the other side of the highway, toward downtown. Spiderholes had been sunk in the Cases' backyard, just in case we tried to tunnel our way out. Under the waters of the Long Island Sound, and off the south shore too, submarines bobbed slightly under the waves. Every plane that passed overhead, even the commercial flights, heck, even the skywriters promising GREAT DEALS, QUOGUE CHEVROLET, were stuffed with air marshals. In a spiral pattern, cutting across Suffolk County, Connecticut, out into The City and even to the tip of Orient Point, where a ferry sometimes goes, there were soldiers, their eyes and guns pointed toward little Weinbergia. Beyond even them, in factories in refineries, good old blue-collar workers bent over their machines and smiled into the spray of sparks spat out of their equipment—overtime, double time, maybe even triple time. And they were all coming for me, fueled and driven on by Geri, my mother, and her nasal shrieking for me on every television screen in the world. "My boy, I want my beautiful boy, home, safe with his mother! Home with me!" she cried out, and her whining landed on the broad backs of the world like a slaver's whip.

And there was nothing I could do about it. I read the minds of the generals, nothing. They'd sewn America up tight. I checked the military minds of foreign powers—the only option in North Korean dreams was pulling the trigger on the bomb out on the lawn. Paranoids, the ones with those tin foil hats (they don't work, by the way) and a million back-up plans, they were out of bright ideas. So were the military historians, the Warhammer players, the Dungeons and Dragons nerds, everyone. No one had any answers, except one.

Get used to being pushed around by America.

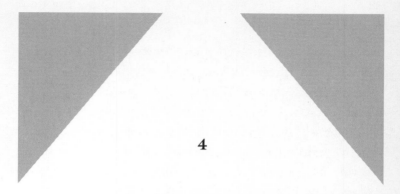

4

Of course, one thing you can do if you're playing chess—and if you're actually playing chess in a dumb movie with a really dramatic script or something—is just kick over the board and declare victory. We didn't kick over the board; everyone else did it for us. Vermont went especially crazy. The counties full of snowy hillbillies that make up what they call the Northeast Kingdom declared itself a literal kingdom, and the towns of Brattleboro and Marlboro seceded, formed a pair of communes, and then merged into one city-state. But that was Vermont, so nobody really noticed except that Unilever issued a press release stating that Ben & Jerry's ice cream production wouldn't be affected, and the US sent some troops to make sure none of the highways were blocked by either the hippies or the rednecks.

The bigger news was the explosion, of course. Gray McGrath, who owned a big farm in Springettsbury Township, Pennsylvania, didn't have a nuclear bomb, but he had plenty of gasoline and fertilizer, and a few handy flatbeds on which to arrange the stuff on the borders of his acreage. He announced that his farm was seceding from the US and that McGrathia would be a new homeland for "the white race" via his website. He also especially requested "blonde-haired white women," the "proud kind" he said, to report to

McGrathia in order to help "build the race." He even promised to "treat" them "all very nice" especially if they could
show that they were of "French Huguenot extraction." He
was also very worried, he said about "secret Puerto Ricans"
with light skin sneaking into his new country, so there would
be strict "border policing." All those quote marks I'm showing you are annoying, but really, they were all in the press
release, in quotes for no reason, just like that.

Anyway, as you probably saw on the news, McGrathia
exploded when a woman named Lenora Cline—she's black,
not a "secret Puerto Rican"—drove down from York with
nothing but a book of matches and a copy of the local paper
in which she saw the McGrathia story, stopped at his border,
walked right up to him (the dog was barking, McGrath was
too flummoxed to even call her the n-word; he'd never fired
his shotgun at anyone before and was afraid), turned the
paper into a torch, and tossed it at a wagon full of kerosene-
drenched fertilizer. She got blown across the street, and her
eyebrows went even farther, and McGrath suffered three
degree burns over much of his body. (The really funny thing
is that McGrath and Cline are like *in love* now; they even
share a hospital room and talk all night long about the country they'll found on an oil rig somewhere with book deal and
insurance money.) The dog lost a leg and was found limping
about half a mile a way, its fur singed, but otherwise happy.
That was the dog Sandra Bullock adopted, remember?

Then there were all the others. Libertopia in Idaho, where
a whole condo complex got together and declared itself a tax-
free capitalist zone—they tried to hold off the troops with a
vial of what they said was anthrax. One of their CEOs, a fel-

low who called himself Glen, but whose real name was Ted (he thought that was "too faggy" for TV), made his declaration public too. After spending forty minutes trying to figure out which side to part his shaggy light brown hair on (he finally decided the "right," because he didn't want to "seem left") he set up a podium in the complex's common room and waved a vial around during their press conference.

"We are all willing to die for our freedom," he explained, "the way the Founding Fathers were willing, the way most Americans, infantilized as they are by the womb-to-tomb nanny state, are no longer willing. But we are, and we shall show through superior competition and the harnessing of individual ingenuity and freedom," and then he dropped the vial.

"Of course we wouldn't endanger ourselves or media professionals gathered here by risking exposure. That was just a prop!" he said, though now he stumbled over his words and kept glancing down at the broken test tube, the white powder spilled across the tasteful beige carpeting. The journalists murmured and silently moved the story from page A3 and the six o'clock lead to after sports and "Pet of the Week."

"We do have anthrax, it was purchased in the free market, which Americans are indoctrinated to believe is a great evil when it is—" and he was interrupted again, this time by the local police, who just beat the crap out of him while the cameras still rolled and then dragged him and his four co-founders away. The cops had been called in by one of the private security guards who wanted to go home and have Sunday dinner with his mother, but couldn't because one of the Libertopians had welded the main gate to the condo complex shut and then blocked it with a big yellow Hummer. "How the hell were those idiots gonna 'free trade' anything with the gate shut?" he wanted to know.

And there were others. The mayor of Bloomington, Indiana, tried to declare independence, only to say that he'd willingly rejoin the United States if the federal government paid off the city's debts. He was recalled. In Texas, four different microstates emerged, and three of them even managed to chase off the local cops, and then set up counter-operations against National Guard sieges. Cincinnati's Gaslight District split off too and managed to even absorb a police presence through a big block party. An all-black nation emerged in one of the neighborhoods of Camden, New Jersey, and cops traded small arms fire with the rebels for most of the afternoon before drawing back. The governor of New Jersey acted upset, but deep down he hoped he'd be able to excise the city altogether and not have to worry about it. He wouldn't even use the New Jersey National Guard and insisted that the Camden problem was a federal matter.

Five squats in Eugene, Oregon, left, as did the homeless of People's Park in Berkeley, California. Somebody declared himself the King of Harlem, but at his press release just shouted "Howard Stern rules! Bababooey Bababooey!" A sandbar in the Connecticut River was claimed by a couple who had built a minigun in their basement. A warehouse turned loft in El Cerrito, California, went rebel too, thanks to the Maoist Labor Party or something like that. (Yes, I read their minds; there was disagreement over their own party name. Very weird. Half that group was FBI agents anyway.)

King Daniel watched it all on TV and just sighed. He didn't

know what to think; his brain was all thumping and semi-famil-
iar flashes, like I was looking at a washing machine full of my
own clothes at a Laundromat. Adrienne prowled around the
couch, wanting to be helpful and useful and looking for some
sex, but my father still loved my mother and missed her too
much. I needed to use the bathroom, but somebody was blog-
ging in there. Outside, across the line, a few trucks growled and
headlights came on. Half the American force was leaving, being
recalled. Kelly and Barry (the whitey white high-fiving guy)
were lured to the window by the noise and ruckus.

"What does it mean?" Kelly asked.

Barry thought that some of the troops might be rede-
ployed due to the rash of microstates that had sprung up.
There was even a college girl from downtown Port Jameson
that had created some kind of wire-mesh hoop skirt, no fab-
ric, just the hoops, and she didn't wear jeans or panties
underneath or anything, and declared herself a roving per-
son-state. She lasted two blocks before tipping over. An
American passerby who had some needlenose pliers rescued
her and ended her great experiment in personal democracy
and public nudity.

There was so much happening: the TV was on, as were
two or three others that new citizens had brought with them.
We had cable and a big Long Island TV, they had staticky
reception and ghostly black-and-white figures, like thumb
prints, telling them the news. Also radios, and laptops everywhere. Almost no typing, just finger-jabs and clicking from
page to page, to find out what we were supposed to have said
today and what the word on the net is about us (Moron of
the day: "Now people are going to think that all Christians

act this way!" Like Dad said, "There's a sentence that contains more errors than words.")

It was hard to think, much less pick out the thoughts of the people around me. Barry was confident, thought he smelled good; he was here to get laid because he read somewhere that hippie chicks put out in crisis situations. Kelly was afraid that she was going to die, and was wondering if she didn't make a big mistake in emigrating to Weinbergia. She was also trying to figure out exactly what to say and how to act so that she could have sex with Barry without it seeming like she was just going with him because they were in a crisis situation.

My father, watching the various special reports cutting in on other special reports, only thought "Good" whenever the cops, the National Guard, or the feds shut down another newly emergent microstate. We were the only ones with neighborhood nuclear superiority. King Daniel was proud. Everyone else? Too busy, buzzing like attic wasps over politics, sleeping arrangements, secret schemes to grab the last can of Coke or yesterday's soggy fishstick. I went upstairs where things were quieter.

But not silent. I was the only kid in all Weinbergia, and the prince besides, so most of our new citizens didn't stake a claim in my room. (Dad had four people in the master bedroom, and slept on a cot like everyone else. The big mattress and box spring had been moved downstairs for a bunch of smelly punk rocker types from Westchester.)

But when I opened the door there were Rich and Adrienne, sitting on the corner of my low twin bed, his arm wrapped around her shoulders, and both of them staring at my screensaver, of all things. They were even murmuring about it ("Oh my, it flickers like that all night?" "No, it stops after ten minutes or so.") and they were even thinking what they said. Usually, when people make empty comments, they're thinking of something else.

"Hello," I said.

"Hey chief," Rich said brightly. Adrienne smiled the lady's smile for kids.

"I'm going to use my computer now," I said. "No more screensaver, okay?" I slid into my seat and tapped the mouse. They shifted on their butts a bit, but didn't move.

"Do you mind if we stay here and, uhm, hang out with you, Herbie?" Adrienne acted as though she had never said the words "hang out" before in her entire life.

I told her it was fine and Rich asked what I planned to do. "Some neat video game? Update a website? Talk to your little girlfriend on Instant Messenger? Send some emails?"

"I like to look at pornography on my computer."

Rich suddenly flashed to an image of some porno he had seen, so I obliged by typing "barely legal anal" into the search engine that's on my browser's start page. "It's very healthy, you know, for young boys like me. We try to shed our old-fashioned American sex hang-ups here in Weinbergia. That's why I look at porn for two or three hours before I go to sleep on that bed you two are sitting on every night."

"Well, that's just great," Adrienne said. She didn't think it was great at all. "I think I'll talk health and family services policy with your father." With that she got up and didn't even glance at Rich as she left, taking three quarters of the air in the room with her.

"So, uh—" Rich said and I clicked the Search button and

my screen filled with thumbnails of women who certainly
weren't barely legal, stacked like sandwiches with men as the
bread. Sweat burst from Rich like he was a crushed grape.
Then I shut the browser window.

"Oh-kay then," he said.

"Oh-kay," I said.

He stared at me for a long time; if he was thinking it was
on some weird weatherman-reptile level that didn't translate
into words or even images. Then he said, "You know a lot of
things, Herb."

I shrugged.

"Do you know why the troops are pulling out?"

"Well, only some of 'em are."

He ran his fingers through his hair, and huffed. "Yes, but
the ones that are pulling out, do you know why they are
pulling out?"

I actually didn't, since even the troops who were leaving
didn't know why they were, or where they were going, or
what would happen next. Most of them were just glad to be
moving away from the garden gnome nuke, but worried that
they'd end up in Iran or Brazil or some other hotter spot on
the map. Maybe Providence, Rhode Island. Brown University
was supposedly planning to secede next. I went a bit deeper,
into some dark mind in some dark basement. All Rich saw was
my eyes peering up at the ceiling, tongue on my lips, like I
was trying to think of something good.

"They're worried that vibrations and movements of soldiers and material on the front might jostle something here,
and bring the radioactive bits of the nuke close enough to
start the fissioning process."

I had no idea where all the blood in Rich had rushed, but he didn't seem to have any of it anymore. Maybe his feet were red as stoplights. "You mean, kill everyone?" I didn't want to say yes, so I turned back to my computer. The screensaver was back, with spidery lines of purple and green. It was pretty interesting, after all.

"I heard something, too. I have friends, been getting a few tips here and there, strictly nfa. That's 'not for attribution,' you know, so I can't say who. Uhm, not that you'd know who they were anyway." At that moment, I did.

"You know, you're big news in the outside world, Herbie. You should check out a site when you're done with your po— pictures. Mysonherbiethelovebug.org." Then Rich got up, squeezed my shoulder, and walked off without another word. The door to my bedroom opened to a roar of light and ciga-rette smoke and nervous smells, then closed again, but all the fog of the outside world remained here with me.

I typed in the URL and looked at the site. It took forever to load, because the designer didn't really know what she was doing. There was a big old gif of me, a few years ago. I was missing a front tooth in the photo, though I remembered that when that picture had actually been taken I had my teeth. Photoshop, to make me look more innocent or more pathetic or something. There was a link to an online petition addressed to my Dad, who was called "a good man who had done one terrible, terrible, thing."

There was no news of Weinbergia. As far as visitors to the website knew, Rich Pazzaro was tied up in the basement, lit-erally chained to the furnace, and Dad and I were sitting up in our living room alone, in our underwear and in the dark, inventing nonsense languages and scraping the bottom of our last jar of Skippy with our dirty, overgrown nails, to keep alive, "all for the sake of Daniel Weinberg's quixotic quest," to read the website copy's version of the tale.

And I checked the newsfeeds on my other browser, then I checked your minds. Yes, even yours. And most of you knew nothing of the steady stream of people taking our side, coming here with nothing but the clothes on their backs and all the money they could pull out of a gas station ATM, swearing their oaths to Weinbergia, looking to start a new life. All you knew was what Geri had told you, what some talking heads described as the inevitable nuclear holocaust brewing on Long Island's North Shore, of the day-thick traffic jams on the L. I. E. and the Northern State, and of the Klansmen and anarchists who suddenly started arming themselves, for no reason at all other than that they hated freedom and democracy. Because they had previously been given too much of it all at once.

I generally kept my speakers down, but saw a little dancing musical note on the bottom of the front page and when I turned up the volume heard that Mom had a beepy-boopy MIDI version of "You Light Up My Life" playing in a continuous loop on the page, and there was no way to turn it off or to turn the volume down on the webpage.

So now, it really was war. I packed a bag and waited for the morning.

5

I had hopes that they'd come for me subtly. Send in another spy, maybe Tanya Levine, who'd cry and bring me some American candy—lots of Weinbergians were anti-sugar all of a sudden; nothing but that awful candied fruit nobody likes had been offered for a couple of days (I blame the hippies)—and ask me to go back with her to visit Mom, just for a bit, just for a little bit. Then I'd be hit over the head with a black-jack, stuffed into a National Guard truck along with some Meals Ready to Eat and green blankets, and trundled off to Fort Collins, Colorado (where my maternal grandma lives), or wherever for a flashbulb-heavy reunion with Mom.

But once they had cleared the front of the great rumbly trucks and Armored Personnel Carriers that might have acci-dentally jostled and thus triggered Weinbergia's first and last line of defense, the Army decided to go ninja on us. No con-scious thought was involved in the process at all; it was if they picked their plans out of a bingo tumbler or something. Even I didn't know what happened until the first canister of tear gas came flying through the bay window in the living room.

Breakfast's first shift had just ended. We were eating beans and toast because one of our recent émigrés was British and had a hankering for them, and beans are really cheap and easy to parachute in from a low-flying Piper Cub hired by the

Palau government. The soldiers had blasted three of the cases to hell on the way down, but one had survived, and Disco Barry had fetched it in order to impress some white girl with dredlocks and a trust fund. Her name was Rhiannon and she was happy for the beans and also happy that so many of "our bird friends" were coming to visit us. "A good omen," she said.

The roof was full of seagulls and pigeons picking at beans. Wings flapping, occasional squawks, endless jokes about who was going to go outside first to get the newspaper and risk being splattered by the shower of droppings. Then screams and scrambling and the sting of peppery smoke.

I was lucky. I was in the bathroom when the first canister of crazy purple knockout gas came throw the living room window downstairs. I grabbed the toothpaste and slathered it all over my lips and eyelids, then ran downstairs, threading my way between the people in line for the toilet in the hallway. I whipped it out, you know, *it*, and aimed for the hole on the side of the canister and started peeing right on it, to neutralize the chemicals and stop the reaction. That's how they do it, *intifada*-style, and I'd picked up the trick in a nervous dream the night before. I'd saved Weinbergia.

Then three more canisters came in through three more windows on each end of the house and the screaming started again. I was part of it too. "Dad!" "Dad, help!" He burst out of the basement, nudged aside Kelly, who was already wailing and clutching at her face, and ran to me.

"What do we do?"

"Pee!"

His face blanched. "I just used the downstairs half-bath!"

As one, we turned to what was left of the line of people on the steps. Half of them were wheezing and crumpled, others had run upstairs and kicked open the windows. None of their bladders would be useful either; some of them had already gone in their pants. Two birds fluttered in, then smacked into walls and a flailing guy who had just left the bathroom. Dad wheezed and was suddenly leaning on me, heavily, his knees weak and eyes screwed shut. Tears dripped like sweat from his face. My toothpaste mask was wearing off; I could feel the tingling, my nostrils and bronchial tubes squeezing shut like they'd just been through the coldest winter run ever. I grabbed the remote from Dad's belt and turned to the door to face a trio of soldiers in bug-eyed gasmasks pointing their machine guns at me.

I pointed the remote, antenna-first like it mattered, at them. Their morale broke like a lamp that had just been hit by a basketball, and they walked out, almost stumbling backwards down the narrow porch steps. I stepped out of the house on wobbly legs, and made it about ten feet before falling to me knees. The garden gnome was feet away, its smile egging me on. Its eyes were so bright and blue. Too blue, scary, really, like anything else that doesn't blink. Like all the cameras and headlights on the Hummers and the goggly gas masks worn by the line of soldiers just beyond the curb of my house. But I had the bomb and held the remote high, so everyone could see it, and me. There were cameras; I knew they wouldn't shoot me. I'm still a kid, a white kid they'd been painting as a victim for almost a week, and besides, I was coughing so much, my mouth and lips were full of snot and tears, I was sweating and shaking. I felt some puke bubbling up in the far end of my throat. My thumb might slip.

I could kill us all.

Blind and hoarse, I screamed.

"Mom!"

Needless to say, Dad had other remote controls, stashed here and there around the house. I knew that, but nobody else did (though the military simply assumed he did, and backed off behind their front line when I escaped the gas trap), and I felt like hanging on to the remote I had. Even after I was told that Mom was being helicoptered in to see me. Even after they offered me candy bars, money, a ride in a tank. Or when they threatened to break my f-ing arm or just cut it off with a hacksaw, and my other arm too. And they weren't lying either. They just weren't telling the full truth yet. They wanted to see what would happen when Mom came before doing anything drastic, like shooting my wrist off so quickly I wouldn't have time to depress the button on the remote.

High-level negotiations had taken place, in New York, at the United Nations. Weinbergian windows had been replaced, food stores augmented, international treaties regarding mail, civilian air traffic, and wetlands preservation instituted (we had a disused garden that tended to puddle) and in return they had to send Kelly out to America with a duffle bag full of my clothes. She didn't even try to smile or hide her upset, and wouldn't touch me. She had been rehearsing some inspirational thing to say to me ("Stay strong" or "I love you") but ended up just stammering out "Here, here you go. Here. Your bag to go. Go. Here. Bye."

And she dropped the bag at my feet and all but ran out of the gymnasium.

It took a long time for Geri, my mom, to show up. There were briefings with PsyOps first—they thought I'd have Stockholm Syndrome and thus support my dad. It never even occurred to any of them that they, the US troops, were the ones who kidnapped me. Then Mom's publicist wanted her to change into sweatpants, to look more "homey" and by homey she meant pathetic, but Mom kept her slacks on. She wanted to look nice for me.

When my mother finally came, she looked very different. Her hair had been cut by a real hairdresser, not by herself, in the bathroom mirror, like she usually did it. Her teeth were capped and she was wearing a nice blazer in a color that wasn't quite pink. My mother sizzled with crazy, but it quieted down when she saw me. We were in the gym in the high school, where I had been carried, remote in hand (and yes, I knew it wouldn't work more than a couple hundred yards away from the nuclear device). Soldiers lined the benches, at attention when the cameras were here, but when my mother arrived and they were chased out by Captain Whiting's stiff bark, most of the guys just leaned against the walls and chatted with each other, mostly about how similar this all felt to how they leaned against gymnasium walls, chatting, a couple of years prior when they were all high school students.

We hugged for a long time, not thinking anything at all.

A ping-pong table and two folding chairs on opposite sites had been set up for us. After about two seconds of looking over the tiny net at one another I suggested that we get up and move the chairs so that they'd be against the long sides of the table, and that way we'd be closer. Geri loved the idea and we quickly arranged the seats properly. "You're so clever," she said.

"Cleverer than the Army guys who put the chairs on the wrong end," I said, and watched her fume.

"*Stop*," she said through clenched teeth, "saying bad things about the government." Then "You're just like your father."

"He's fine, by the way."

"That's one way of putting it, I guess. I've had about my fill of your father, and I hope you have too, because I suspect it'll be awhile before you see him again."

I shook my head and slid off the folding chair. "You can't kidnap me. There are rules. International law—"

"Don't be stupid, Herbie!" She was angry, like burnt toast popping right out of the toaster. "This isn't kidnapping, this is you being removed from a dangerous environment. There is *no* country called Weinbergia; I don't care what the United Nations or Palau says." She sat back in her chair, already exhausted. "Palau. God. What right do they have interfering anyway?"

"Well, Palau only gained its independence from the US in 1994. See, it started off as a Spanish holding when the Pope, well, hmm." She wasn't listening.

"It doesn't matter. We're cutting off all financial aid to Palau and Morocco and Italy and all those other little nothing countries that have decided to use your father as a wedge against us."

"Us who? The US? You never talked like this before!"

"And *that* was my mistake. I wanted you to grow up to be

a patriot, Herb, to have a little pride in yourself and your fellow Americans, not to be an annoying know-it-all cynic like your father."

"I'm not a cynic. It's very idealistic, starting a new country, opening doors to the tired and hungry yearning to breathe free."

Mom put her elbows on the table and ignored the wobble as she buried her head in her hands. "Let's just go home," she said, and of course she meant to Colorado, where she had a new garden apartment with a small microwave where she warmed up her frozen dinners and a satellite dish where she spent eighteen hours a day watching Weinbergia, hoping to catch a glance of me or my silhouette in one of the windows. (We generally kept the shades drawn, due to the number of new citizens who liked to walk around naked on whichever floor I wasn't on at the moment.)

"Weinbergia is my home."

"You're *not* going back to that house."

"Then I'll go live with the poor people in the dump."

She sneered at that, more disgusted with me than I would have ever thought possible. "My son, the doctor," she said. "I'm your mother, I have custody, we're going home, and if you want to stay here and have a tantrum I'll have the guards throw you on an Army helicopter to get you home if I have to."

And that's the story of my first-ever trip in an Army helicopter.

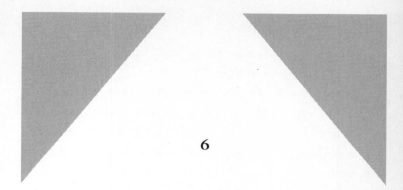

6

The worst thing about my mother's house in Colorado was that Colorado is still in America. Also, you need a car to get anywhere. My mother even drove down to the private road that surrounds the complex to pick up her mail from the boxes on the corner of her block.

I was being "homeschooled" by Mom, which meant that she'd watch me fill out workbooks and I'd occasionally ask her a question I knew she couldn't answer in order to let me use the computer. There were all sorts of parental controls on her box too, but of course it was easy to learn her passwords with a little telepathy so I was back online. I didn't feel like writing very much though, and instead just read the various headlines about Weinbergia and checked out some of the hatesites that have sprung up about it.

That's the funny thing that Daniel and the Weinbergians never seemed to get. They were always so worried about propaganda and media—which is why Richard wasn't just depantsed and thrown over enemy lines in the middle of the night—but the media doesn't matter at all. People instantly go totally crazy when you build a nuke and start your own country; there's no need for the networks to spin it. They're all trained to distrust the new idea, the individual initiative that has nothing to do with making a zillion dollars or being in movies, the idea that someone might just announce, "I'm not part of you guys, so there!"

I know this not only because you're all open books to me, but because my workbook told me so. The Social Studies unit was on immigration – my job was to find an immigrant and interview him or her about coming to America. I had to fill out this sheet explaining Five Reasons Why Your Immigrant—*my immigrant?*—Left His Or Her Home Country and Five Reasons Why He or She Likes America. Then I had to get a picture of something that my immigrant thinks represents America and paste it into the workbook. Well, the only immigrant I knew was myself, so here's what I filled out:

Five Reasons Your Immigrant Left His Or Her Home Country

1. I was overcome by crazy purple knockout gas.
2. Long lines for the bathroom.
3. All the adults around me started saying things like "make love" when they thought I was in earshot, and that's one creepy phrase.
4. China didn't kidnap me first.
5. I was too scared to push the button.

Five Reasons Your Immigrant Likes America

1. I'd *better* like it.
2. Life's a bit easier under America's domestic policy than it is under its foreign policy, let me tell you.

3. My mom lives here.
4. It's where they hold Wrestlemania every Spring.
5. Mostly I like that it's fraying at the edges, and that all these other countries are popping up out of nowhere. I think that's a good sign, and it's really nice of America not to just randomly kill anyone and everyone who tries it, at least not right away. Thanks.

And for my picture of America, I found one on the net, on some freebie angelfire.com webpage by some guy who used to be a Marine or really likes the Marines or his brother was a Marine or something (it really wasn't clear which). It was a photo of my father, in his shorts, his mouth shaped like a big O and his forehead glistening from sweat as he leans into the steering bar of his lawn mower. There were two captions on the pic too, in big red computery font letters. FUELED BY MARX says the caption up top, and on the bottom of the photo, RULED BY SATAN.

Bored, I went to the fridge. A half-empty jar of Best Foods mayonnaise and an old sock were in it. I can't even imagine how my mother ended up with those two items and nothing else in her refrigerator, and I'm a mind-reader. Best Foods. God. It's the same company as Hellman's back in New York, but out here, in the West, they call it Best Foods.

Maybe, I thought, *I should change my name from Herbert Weinberg to "Handsome" Johnny Stryker or something like that.*

In Weinbergia, the fridge was always full. Cuban sandwiches (from Cuba!), Chinese food (from Hunan Gardens, in the King Kullen strip mall across Route 347, on the Southern frontier), crazy hippie green stuff, ice cream bars, lots of

chicken cooked in all sorts of ways. You name it. In
Weinbergia, I always had some company, if only because people would come up to me in little groups or two and threes,
to marvel at the Smarty Kid who didn't wear a backwards
baseball cap and let his jaw drop to his nipples as a matter of
course.

And I guess that's why it was such a big deal that dad built
a nuke too. After my kidnapping, the news sort of petered
out, even though Weinbergia is still ringed by foreign troops,
and even though the garden gnome is still ticking out on the
lawn. Weinbergia is just fodder for various Internet nerds and
political science and law school students writing their papers.
At least the weather has turned now, so there's no need for
Dad to mow the lawn. Portuguese UN peacekeepers did the
raking, which was over pretty quickly because the gas attack
defoliated both the trees in my yard. My mother became the
new celebrity, what with the TV appearances and "the book"
about her brave struggle to reclaim me. Geri was so naïve; she
actually wrote the first ten pages herself and gave them to an
agent. The first page is hanging on a bulletin board at the
publishing house, because the first paragraph reads like this:

I knew that I had to rescue my loving pure little innocent
son from the dastardly clutches of my diabolical husband
because I love my little Herbert so very much and nobody
else could love him like I did. My husband who is mentally
ill and now I realize has been for years ever since that time
during Christmas shopping three years ago when he tore
open a twelve-pack of toiler paper at the Wal-Mart and
grabbed three rolls and flung them over the shelves into the

next aisle while he hysterically screamed madly "Hey-o! Heads up!" When he began to secretly skulk around in the shadows in broad daylight I knew I had a battle for my life and the life of my loving son in my hands and that I would do anything to protect my innocent child from the world, which is full of unknown dangers.

The rest they shredded, thank God. Geri spent a lot of the time she was actually home talking to and emailing the ghost-writer. She ate most of her suppers out as well, but was always happy to bring home "doggie bags"—*Gee, thanks Mom! Love, The Dog*—from Wolfgang Puck's place or wherever she'd been treated that night.

I had little else to do with my days but allow my mind to drift, all the way back to Weinbergia. Weinbergia, where Rich was leading a daring commando mission over the wire and into enemy territory, namely, the Qool Mart about half a mile into American territory.

"I just can't get them out of my head," Rich said. "I haven't had a Cuebar since I was a kid. They have those four little rectangular sections: caramel, coconut, peanut butter, and strawberry." My father was just staring at him, but a couple of folks littering the dining room, on pillows or half-rolled up and wrinkled sleeping bags, nodded. Then there was Adrienne, who felt like she was in a commercial, because she was.

"It's only one klick down to the Qool Mart. We should make a move."

"We?" asked Barry. "Besides, candy is never as good as you remember it from when you were a kid."

"The corporations," Rhiannon said, and murmurs of agreement rose up from the crowded room. Coups in Haiti, mass production, the decline in union labor in factories, the fact that milk chocolate doesn't melt as quickly as dark when loaded into trucks—that's why chocolate stinks these days, except for the expensive stuff. It's amazing what people think they know.

Richard leaned in, his elbows balanced oddly on the arms of the chair in which he said. "You know we need to make a move, Daniel. Do something. People need a new adventure to focus on. You know, make the front page, over the fold, again." He leaned back in his chair, held out his arms, then brought his hands together so that his index fingers and thumbs met, making a little cube-y shape. "Cuuuuuue-bar" he said, just like the voice over guy from the commercials used to.

Dad glanced around for a second, then reached for the glass sugar bowl and turned it over. Along with a cascade of white sugar fell a little black video camera, a new type hardly bigger than a roll of 35 mm film. He snatched it up, stomped out of the dining room and up the steps, shouldered his way through the knot of people always milling right outside the bathroom door, yanked the door open, ignored the shriek and flailing of legs and panties stretched between white knees as some woman named Elly rushed to stand and cover herself, and flushed the camera. He nearly broke the handle to the toilet.

The screaming and flailing about—Weinbergians like to speak with their hands because of the close quarters, a little flick of a finger can mean a lot once you catch someone's eye—clicked off like a television when my mother barged in to the living room, her hands full of big white shopping bags. She bought me a whole new wardrobe. Sweaters, which I hate to wear, "but you're in Colorado now and it gets a lot colder here," five pairs of shoes, all the same but in different sizes, because "one will fit and you'll grow into at least one of the sizes; the rest we can return," and slacks slacks slacks. No jeans. "It's time to grow up," she said. She was wearing jeans though. The last bag held three plastic domes holding roasted chickens from the fancy supermarket. I called them pheasant under glass and got a dirty look instead of a polite chuckle. I'm not so clever anymore, now that Mom has to look at me every day between photo opportunities and psychological assessments.

We ate a chicken, and salad out of a bag. Mom didn't even pour all the leaves and whatever out onto our plates; we just leaned over the table like Weinbergian hippies and jabbed at the veggies with our forks.

"So, what did you do all day?" she asked me.

"I dunno," I said. "What did you do all day?"

Mom dropped her fork. "I went shopping. I had a meeting. *With a Senator*. I made some phone calls." She sighed.

"Where?"

"Cell phone."

"Oh. Who did you talk to?"

"Oh, *Vanity Fair*, some freelance writer from the *New Times*, that sort of thing." She frowned, thinking. I peeked.

"Still haven't heard anything from *People*, huh?"

"No!" Her hands contracted into tight little fists. "Can you believe it? I even faxed them." She couldn't even look at me, she was so disgusted. She turned back to me finally. "I faxed them twice today alone. I was worried about time zones. I don't know if I'll ever get used to Mountain.

"When *People* does call, they'll probably want to take our picture. That's why I bought you seven sweaters. You should keep the orange one at hand in case they call us tomorrow."

I smiled. "Sure, Mom!" We ate in silence, while she fantasized about a handsome, flat-stomached photojournalist sweeping her off her feet and winning me over with lots of hair-tousling and non-molesting wrestling lessons. A *People* photojournalist. That way, no politics.

About six hours later, my father was staring at the ceiling in his dark room when he shifted to his side and peered over the edge of his bed at a few of the shadowy figures who took up the floor space in their bags and blankets.

"Who wants to come to Qool Mart with me?" he asked. "This sounds stupid, but I can't get those damn Cuebars out of my head." The shadows on the floor shifted and groaned like a talkative fog. Dad reached down and poked the mass, tapping shoulders (or foreheads, an ankle, a big fleshy something that he thought was a belly but worried was a boob, which would create a national crisis or, even worse, some horrible and lengthy lesbian "processing session" at breakfast) and rousing his confederates. "Feet," he said softly as he sat up and swung around to get off the bed. A few shapeless blobs rose up and sprouted limbs.

"Cuebar, let's do this thang," Barry said.

"Should we…get Rich?" asked Adrienne in a quiet sleepy voice, which came…

Which came from the side of the bed my mother used to sleep on. I hadn't sensed her till she awoke.

She was in bed with my father. In bed. They had been almost doing things. Almost, so quiet, hardly a squeak, just hands and the tips of their fingers, down below. They were really tired, but with all the rolling over and the like on the floor, King Daniel couldn't help but wake up, his brain a fog, having forgotten why he couldn't have sex with the woman in the bed with him. For her part, Adrienne was happy to lie there and "be pleasured."

She used the words *be pleasured*. Mentally. Dinner came up my throat and I ran to the bathroom to stare into the toilet for a long time, waiting. Once, either my father or my mother would come and comfort me. Back in Port Jameson, they were always so attuned to me, like they could read my mind. I've always wanted to meet someone who could do that, but as far as I knew then, I was the only telepathic person in the whole world.

I pushed Adrienne out of my mind, and concentrated on Dad. He and a small knot of Weinbergians—and yeah, Adrienne was among them, but to me she was nothing but a silhouette, a black blotch on the lawn—approached the border, giddy with anticipation. Sometimes, you can even look forward to maybe being shot, if it involves the promise of a little road trip to a convenience store. Exciting stuff; they have everything at those stores: Froot Loops, push-brooms, coffee, magazines that promise six-pack abs with a single push-up, maps of the world (Palau, here we come!), and Cuebars.

"Hi," my father said, so sure of himself that he wasn't even thinking. A soldier looked at him like he was the dreamy remnant of an incomplete nap.

"What?"

"We're coming through."

"Uhm," the soldier said, "I don't think you can do that. I mean, I'll have to radio up the chain of command."

"Why? Just let us through." The Weinbergians nodded. One of them had made a passport with a portable laser printer and an old Polaroid camera he had found at the bottom of the junk closet. "Where are you from?" Dad asked.

"I grew up in Spanish Harlem."

"Dicey area."

The soldier shrugged.

"But you were allowed to go where you wanted, right? Sure, someone could say 'Get off my turf—'"

"Heh," the soldier said, "I only ever heard the word turf on TV."

"Yeah yeah, but anyway, here's the thing, there was animosity, but you were allowed to travel wherever you liked. We're not under arrest or anything, we're not being detained in my house, we're just ordinary Ameri—"

"Nah, you ain't, remember? Weinbergia." The soldier smiled. He liked to be clever, and his job didn't really offer much call for it.

Dad shrugged. "Okay," he said, "we declare the hostilities over. Mission accomplished! Say, good job, soldier, for resolving all this. You'll probably get a medal, maybe even a stamp with your picture on it one day." Behind him, a Weinbergian passport was torn to shreds by its enthusiastic owner. Dad stepped forward and, careful not to nudge or touch the soldier, but with his hands out to direct him, crossed the border.

Adrienne and the others followed, nervously. Dad smiled and waved as he picked his way across the driveway. Jake, the guy who carried the passport, accidentally stubbed his toe on a tank tread, but the gunner didn't notice thanks to the iPod some Support the Troops campaign had sent everyone.

I hoped someone would stop them. By shooting Adrienne.

Dad made it to the corner of the block, turned and led his band down Route 25A. Adrienne took his arm because the shoulder of the road isn't designed for walking—everyone on Long Island drives everywhere—and was full of sand, dead leaves she thought were spiders, and rocks that were conspiring to make her twist her ankle.

You know, she doesn't even like Cuebars.

A car zipped by and its passengers yelled something unintelligible to my dad, who jumped, startled. Adrienne's nails dug into his forearm.

"What was that?"

"What did they say?"

"I dunno!" said Jake.

"Didn't you hear?" asked Adrienne.

"No, why would I? Did you?"

"No!"

"Well then," said Barry.

"Well then what?" said Adrienne.

In the darkness, everyone shrugged and walked on.

What the driver of the car, whose name was Paul DeMello and who worked in Port Jameson for his father who had a vinyl siding business said was, "Aaaah, you're poor! Fucker!" He did this because on Long Island, everybody drives, except for the occasional poor person who somehow managed to find a place to live, in a tiny studio apartment, or even doubled up with someone. And it really drives Paul nuts to see someone dragging their ass along the shoulder of the road, because he feels the need to slow down so he won't hit them, and who knows, sometime somebody, especially a "moulie," might jump in front of his car and sue him for a million dollars after causing the accident. (By *moulie* , Paul who actually thinks of himself as "Paulie," means to think "black guy," but "bad," because moulie is short for *mulignane* which he's been told is similar to the Italian word for eggplant, and anyway his father used to call black people on TV moulies, especially if they led to gambling losses by their poor play on the football field or basketball court. Anyway, he's a jerk, but I think it's funny that "Paulie" and "moulie" kind of sound similar.) And he also gets mad because he works really hard all day, doing vinyl siding, and if he works so hard why can't these people who walk around like apes just work hard too and get a damn car?

Well, Paul doesn't know. Paul doesn't even know why he occasionally sees a tank trundle down his street these days either, because he doesn't like the news and he doesn't talk to too many people these days, not since his girlfriend Tammy dumped him because she doesn't like being screamed at, especially not in front of her own mother like he did that one time in the parking lot of the deli when it was her cousin's Confirmation and they were sent to pick up an eight-foot hero sandwich. So he's never heard of Weinbergia and he doesn't know that he's in the red ring of instant vaporization if the nuke goes up. He'd really be pissed off if he did.

The next car, a military Hummer that was disguised as a civilian vehicle with its baby blue paint job and silkscreened unicorn on the side, came up behind Dad and the Weinbergians slowly, its lights dimmed by half-stop gels borrowed from a news crew in exchange for the crew getting a berth and embedded journalists on the mission to end the stand-off once and for all.

Captain Whiting leaned out the window of the vehicle and shouted over the noise of the engine to Dad, saying "Hey! Weinberg! Stop, you're under arrest." The others stopped, but Dad kept walking. Jake and Leif hurried to catch up and bumped into Adrienne, who scowled and yelped at them.

"Diplomatic immunity!" Dad called out, not even turning to face the captain.

"You surrendered!"

"No I didn't," Dad said. There was some underbrush, so he stomped on it forcefully. Ahead, the white sign of the Qool Mart illuminated the four-car parking lot like a little moon.

"I have a soldier and video says you did, son!"

Dad still didn't stop, still didn't turn. Adrienne huffed after him, upset that she was being reduced to a bit part in the moment with every stride my father pulled ahead. Barry and Jake decided to pace the Hummer, trotting behind it as if they'd be able to hop onto the back, climb in, and subdue everyone involved with all the ninja moves they didn't actually know. But Leif felt strangely confident, giddy. Like he did when he had first emigrated. History was happening. Jake wondered if he shouldn't have saved his passport for eBay.

"No, I said I was ending hostilities. But I also declare victory," Dad said as he finally stopped and turned on his heel to point a thick finger at the captain. "That means you surrender!"

"Okay—wait, no!" From inside the Hummer came a high girly laugh. Whiting craned his neck to frown, and then turned back to Dad. The Hummer idled on the street right outside the Qool Mart as Dad, followed a few steps by Adrienne, stepped onto the asphalt.

"Don't be juvenile, Weinberg. You messed up, big time. I can shoot you right now."

A huge spotlight, which had been left on the roof unused since the Qool Mart opened back in the springtime, sparked to life and flooded the Hummer with a blazing beam. Whiting threw up his arm and squinted. Moths fluttered about, mad from the light. And a voice, lilting and foreign, declared from a tinny PA system, "No you cannot! This man is in my parking lot, the territory of the Islamic Republic of Qool Mart Store No. 351, and any violence on the part of imperialist American aggressors will be answered a thousandfold!"

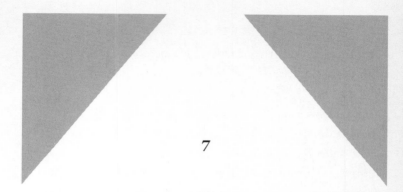

7

My mother likes to wake me up in the middle of the night, because she misses me so much and she doesn't want to be without me, plus she is easily made tipsy on white wine, which she loves and which her new admirers give her all the time. She's like a cloud of perfume and cough medicine, drifting in a windy sky, when she wakes me. Her mind, her scent, all of it. She says, "Love Bug, oh Love Bug," and brushes my hair with her fingers every time. I always try to stay asleep, but it never works. I blaze awake but hold my eyes shut to keep up the illusion, like a guy in prison hiding in the corner of the cell when the guard comes in. All boxed in. She did this now, as I was watching an international incident unfold.

I missed Captain Whiting's barked curses and quick scatter of footsteps guided by rote drilling rather than thought that rushed out into the parking lot. When the spotlight died to a little orange spark, the Hummer was doomed. Propane tanks, set with detonators made from duct tape and clock radios were positioned under all the doors and wheels. King Dad and his followers were surrounded too, by three Qool Mart employees in red and white striped shirts and off-the-rack sunglasses. One of them, his name Umer (though his name tag read *Mark*), wore big novelty sunglasses with pink frames and smiled at my father. He held his arm out toward the door of the Qool Mart and said, "Please, please, come in."

Mom said over and over, "Love Bug, my Love Bug," but her tone was weird as was her own experience of sitting on the corner of my bed, her arm reaching for me as tenderly as Umer's did toward the entrance of the Qool Mart. She wasn't looking at me through her eyes, but just saw the grayish-black blob of my shadowed face. What she saw, in her mind's eye, was herself at the edge of a neater-looking bed, with her clothes fitting better than they really do, caressing a superior version of me. Me, but not so portly, me who had the haircut the *Today Show* wanted me to get. Me, who was thrilled to be free from my psychotic father and his war criminal ways.

"We're out of Cuebars," explained Musad, the franchisee of the Qool Mart, and the Bey of the Islamic Republic of Qool Mart Store No. 351. "We couldn't keep them in stock at all today, thanks to the mention on the television." Musad's nametag read *Sam*. He wasn't wearing sunglasses, which gave him a special look given that all the other employees were— he was the Bey, and they were the Secret Service or something. Even Dad was impressed. "But," said Musad, "I do think we have a product you'd be interested in, if you know what I mean." Musad was sure that Dad did, especially after Dad mimicked the smile and sly tilt of the head Musad performed, but really, Dad had no idea what he was getting into.

Adrienne scowled; she hated Arabs because she heard that back in their home countries they treat women very poorly, wrapping them up in headscarves or even full-length hijabs, and then squeezing their butts and boobs in the marketplaces while the women are trying to shop for their families. And she liked the idea of being handled too much to feel comfortable among so many of them, especially as she couldn't tell whether or not they were undressing her with their eyes.

Barry and Jake busied themselves getting beer and crushed ice.

Mom, all inspired, left my room and sat down to her new laptop, where she checked her email, and answered a few from well-wishers. She used to write back to everyone, but recently got a little jaded. Any mail that mentions Jesus Christ or contains more than four exclamation points (or two right next to each other) she finally decided to ignore after getting way too many of them. She liked what she calls Geri's Generic God. Letters from Christians and Jews and Buddhists and pagans all offered up God's good will, but it could be any God at all. The Generic God, Geri talked to all the time now. About me. ("Will my little boy be okay through all of this?") About Dad. ("What happened?") About tomorrow. ("Please please please make Oprah call tomorrow, or at least Regis.")

Captain Whiting burst into the Qool Mart, sidearm drawn and his arm raised. He waved the gun around till the barrel looked like it was made of rubber. "You're all under arrest!" he shouted. Umer was on him in a flash, his mop handle slamming hard against Whiting's forearm. The gun fell and was kicked across the slick floor. The second blow landed right on Whiting's head, and then as Whiting's guards began running to the door, Umer slid the mop handle through the looped handles of the double doors, wedging them shut. He turned the little sign hanging from one of the handles around so from the outside it read CLOSED. Then he just stood there and smiled as an anxious soldier hefted his rifle and fired a shot into the bulletproof glass of the store. They scattered at the ricochet.

Whiting got to his feet and held up a palm. "No," he barked to the soldiers outside. "Hold your fire! Back to the vehicle!" He turned, wincing and with his hand now to the tender part of his head. "What's going on here? Do you realize that we'll have a Black Hawk down here in three minutes? Who has my gun?" There was a tap on the glass. Everyone turned, and a soldier looked at his captain and shrugged, confused.

Umer said, "The glass is thick. He cannot hear you easily. And the report of the rifle is probably ringing in his ears."

Whiting grunted, then stepped up the glass and cupped his hands around his mouth. "Go back to THE HUMMER!" he yelled, "AND WAIT!" The soldiers nodded and started to walk back, but then Whiting remembered something and started banging on the glass. They turned and Whiting cupped his hands again and shouted, "Private Wallace! I want you to REMOVE THE MUDFLAPS—" Wallace, the soldier who had fired, then knocked, shrugged, and shook his head, so Whiting pointed at the rear of the Hummer, and said even louder, "THOSE ERMINE MUDFLAPS are private issue! THEY'RE MINE!" The soldier, Wallace, smiled widely and nodded, finally understanding. "Take THE MUDFLAPS back to THE STAGING ZONE, Wallace!" He waved, "And the REST OF YOU, stay by THE HUMMER and DON'T try to DEFUSE anything!"

Whiting turned back to the assembled employees and Weinbergians, who were staring. "What? They're sentimental. And I bought them out of my own pocket. You need to do that sometimes. It cheers you up to decorate your own Hummer. It's like a home away from home." Barry understood him at least. He sighed, not thinking anything he wasn't saying, which is really strange for an adult. "So, who has my gun?"

From the back of the room came a voice familiar to local TV news watchers. "I do," said Rich, standing up from his hiding place behind a display case full of old doughnuts. In one hand was Whiting's gun, and in the other, a Cuebar. He was thinking Pulitzer, and about how, when he went to journalism school he learned that Pulitzer was pronounced "Pull it, sir," and not "Pewlitzer."

At just that moment, in the next room over from where I couldn't sleep, my mother began to have a religious experience. Religious experiences are pretty common, actually. I had to teach myself to tune them out when I was a kid, because they're like...hard to explain. Ever see a movie or something on TV where they record a flower or a city all night and then speed up all the frames so it looks like blooms are exploding, cars speed up into red and white squiggles of light, clouds roll under the sky like we were all on a planet-sized roller coaster? It's like watching all those things at once, and being all those things at once. Imagine smelling all those flowers and being sniffed by a giant nose.

Oh, and there is no God, of course. Religious experiences are just a weird thing that happens in people's brains. It's actually the exact opposite of getting a song stuck in your head. You really have to be telepathic to understand what I mean.

The eye of Geri's Generic God manifested itself at the top of her vision. She saw the ceiling separate from the walls of the room and like the sun the Eye peered at her, a giant, inquisitive It. She felt herself rising from her seat, chest first, arms and shoulders thrown back like she was nineteen and being carried to the lifeguards at Lake Ronkonkoma after being discovered in the water by her boyfriend. My mother almost died that day, and her brain starved for thirty seconds. She's been vulnerable to religious experiences ever since then, but never had one till she clicked shut her email and accidentally fired up the wrong screen saver—one she'd never seen before—on her computer. The wavy red into blue with a bright white blob in the middle triggered her.

Now Geri hallucinated that from her perch in the grip of her own Generic God she looked down and saw her body, slumped forward, forehead pressed heavily against the screen of the laptop, which made the edge of the keyboard rise up. Geri wasn't worried about her new machine though; she had transcended material concerns. Then she turned away from her empty body doll and turned to make eye contact with It. Mom stared into the sun-like eye of her Generic God and became It.

From there, it was the usual. All religions have some essential wisdom to share, but unscrupulous men and the pleasures of wealth obscured the message. All of us have a little of God in us, thus we are all one, and should be unified in peace and brotherhood. All we need to do is treat others in the ways in which we want to be treated. God is nature, and nature is

God, so we must stop polluting the Earth. Everyone deserves a full stomach and a warm hug. We should never die alone. An angel watches over each one of us, keeping us from harm. Everything happens for the best, even death, as our own bodies become the flowers of the next generation.

"I, uh, brought this one with me," Rich said of his Cuebar. He was also wearing a t-shirt with the Cuebar logo on it.

Adrienne said "Great. So now what are we supposed to do? We'll probably be arrested if we try to get back home." She glared at Dad.

"Actually, orders on the border are to shoot," said Captain Whiting. Dad glared at him. Not knowing what else to do, Whiting glared at Umer for a moment, but Umer's sunglasses made that unsatisfying, so he tuned to Musad, who had moved from behind the cash register to behind the hot dog warmer, and glared at him. Jake glared at Rich. Barry just put the bags of ice back in the freezer; this was going to take a while, like one of those horrible hour-long pre-meetings his old boss would have before the real, three-hour, meeting. And he had come to Weinbergia to escape.

Musad, his hand in a glove, took a large hotdog—one of those foot-long Qool Dogs that are really kind of gross because they're also like three inches around; too much meat—put it in a bun, and offered it to my father. He took it gingerly, not really thinking. His nervous system was doing all the work. The bloom of confidence in his chest that made him get up and tromp out of his own country was gone, and what replaced it was nothing. No fear, but no thought either. A hotdog was as good as a Cuebar until he bit into it and frowned.

"What?" Adrienne asked. Dad clenched his teeth and pulled from the hotdog a piece of paper, tightly rolled up.

"Hold this," he said of the hotdog to Adrienne, who wouldn't. Jake turned and did. Dad found the edge of the paper with his thumb and carefully unrolled it, then quietly read the peace treaty to himself. In the corner, Rich thought, *Yes!*

Geri's Generic God was all *yes*. There was no hesitation: yes yes yes yes yes. Flowers are beautiful. The universe is a large and wonderful place. There was no room for a Generic Devil or even any explanation for the bad things in the world, like all those people who have been killed by Daisy Cutter bombs, tortured in camps, beaten to death by their parents…well, those things just happen so that Geri can understand how precious life is. Daniel might have beaten me to death, or maybe *his new girlfriend would have*. If not beaten, then maybe I would have been locked in the bathroom and forced to drink from the toilet, or abandoned to the crabgrass on Weinbergia's Eastern frontier, or maybe even sent over to the Cases', where they eat spaghetti out of a can.

That's what brought her back. Me, her precious Love Bug, face smeared with sauce too bright red to be tomato, sitting on a stool at the counter in the Case kitchen, holding an ice cream scoop over the rim of a huge cafeteria-grade can of "prefab" pasta. The glories of life and universe, debased by factory pasta. It was as she awoke that Mom realized that her entire life had been a fraud and a failure. She had never really lived, not since that day when she had enjoyed the cold dark waters of Lake Ronkonkoma for a few seconds too long. She needed to reconnect with nature, to reclaim her wild, primitive self, to transform herself from media figure of the moment ("I think my book might suck" was her first coherent thought upon awakening) and back into Woman. Mother. Eve.

Her head still throbbing as though she had just been awoken from an incomplete nap by a telemarketer phone call, my mother ran around the bedroom, dragging out her luggage and yanking her clothes out of the dresser and closets. It was time for us to move on again, but she wasn't packing for a trip. She was packing to burn.

"Five years…peace between Weinbergia and the entire Muslim world, as vouchsafed and guaranteed by the Islamic Republic of Qool Mart," Dad read aloud.

"Wait a minute," said Whiting, "these people don't speak for the Muslim world."

"Hyah," said Barry. "He's got a point there." Barry hoped making friends with Whiting would get him out of here alive, maybe even without a prison sentence.

Musad said, "Of course I speak for the Muslim world. You, man," he continued, pointing his chin at Barry. "You made it so."

"We have video," Richard said.

Musad reached up to the security monitor and punched a button. The real-time footage on the screen went black and then a moment later was replaced with the same scene, but daylight, with Musad and Barry, only the latter in other clothes, chatting.

Video Barry waved a copy of *Newsday* in Musad's face

and, his voice tinny as a thought from both the mic and the fact that the playback was on the small security speakers, said "Why did your people go crazy this time? Bombing our soldiers just for trying to protect *your* freedom to sell me this newspaper!"

"So, you don't want the newspaper?" Musad-on-tape asked.

It's always strange for me to watch video. I never liked sitcoms, and always hated cartoons, because I could never tell what the characters were thinking. Live shows aren't much better. Reading from a TelePrompter doesn't involve any thinking at all, and bands and dancers and stuff are just constantly mentally counting one-two-three-one-two-three, like that. It's pretty unnerving. Now, Musad was just eerily confident in watching the playback, despite the armored personnel carriers rumbling down Route 25A, despite just being a little island in great big America. Barry was just confused, and starting to get real nervous. He thought of a movie, *The China Syndrome*, and how some guy in it is trying to do something and just gets shot ten times by a machine gun in less than a second. Dying is like exhaling and forgetting to inhale again. Just like that. It could happen. A blink that never ends. He sweated: the lip, the shoulderblades, the crease of his waist against the elastic of his boxers.

He's so gross.

On the video, a gray and fuzzy Barry flails his arms and dives for the jar of beef jerky. Musad pushes him away. Barry swings and falls far short. Umer darts out from the edges of the frame and ties Barry into a full-nelson, then leads him, kicking and thrashing, off the bottom of the screen.

"Well, that's definitive," Adrienne said. She was just a suicide of resentment. *Go ahead*, summed it all up. *Just go ahead.*

"I want a better hot dog, Musad," my father said. "If you know what I mean."

Musad did, and handed Dad a Double Qool With Cheezy Stuff, the hot dog that comes with its own injected American, Swiss, or Pepper Jack cheese. It's also a thrilling eighteen inches long, to hold in all that cheesy goodness.

"Hey," said Jake, a nervous scribble of thought, "why don't you just break this one open and see if there's a better or longer-lasting treaty in it, instead of eating." My father just stared and took a very deliberate bite of the Double Qool, then another. He chewed slow too. Whiting huffed. Barry decided to walk to the corner of the store and put his back against the Big Brapp Frozen Frappucino machine. At least he wouldn't be shot from behind. Dad clenched his teeth and pulled another tightly rolled piece of paper from the center of the dog, where the cheese would have been.

The lights came on. My mother, loud as a volcano, declared, "Love Bug! We have to leave, right now!"

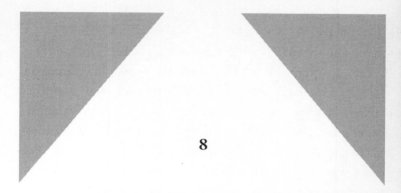

8

My mother wasn't crazy. Well, crazy is relative. It's like static on a radio; sometimes it is louder than the song. She was still thinking loud and rumbly, over the noise of her religious experience. So she was kind of crazy, I guess. No crazier than Dad, whose stoic hot dog munching was pretty much the sanest thing he could do in his situation. For Mom it was the same. Anything that got her away from all the media would probably be a good idea.

Even driving out into a country and finding a flat glacial boulder on which to pile most of our clothes, the laptop, her microwave oven, and some photo albums, to set them all on fire.

"Why the microwave?" I asked, because I knew that mom wanted me to ask.

She clutched it to herself and said, "It's not a natural thing. The only meals that come out tasting anything like they should are meals designed to taste that way only when microwaved. So it's a fake reality disguised as a real imitation. And it takes us away from what we need to experience, what people have done for ten thousand years." She planted it atop a bag I'd opened. Clothes spilled out, but gave the microwave a little cushion to sink into. "Plus, I don't like the beep that goes off when the timer counts down to zero. That isn't natural either. It sounds almost but not quite like a bell."

She squirted lighter fluid over the mass in wild streaks, then stepped back and told me to step back too. She had a book of matches, but the first three didn't take thanks to a little breeze. The fourth stayed lit long enough for Mom to ignite the corner of the book itself. She threw it onto the pile and a web of small flames flared up. The clothes didn't burn that easily, nor did the luggage, but there was a fair amount of black smoke that stung and made me cough a lot. Geri breathed through her mouth hard, willing the fire to really flare up and consume everything. It didn't. The only really exciting bit was when the cord of the microwave melted a bit and almost fell off, but didn't.

"Get back in the car," she said, finally.

We drove without purpose for a long while, down roads so dark that the usual horizon glare from the clusters of gas stations and motels was swallowed by the night. Both of us had floaters in our eyes from staring at the fire, but there wasn't a lot of traffic so it was okay, except that we were running out of gas, and Mom, still on her religious high, was sure that we'd pull up, exhaust sputtering and clutch freezing, at exactly the place the universe wanted us to be.

I guess, by definition, she was right, since every action is a caused action and there is no such thing as free will. (It's true; I checked. Every little thing we do or think is a response and reaction to something else—minds are like the white ball in a game of pool.)

It was a Qool Mart.

The best part about Qool Marts is that time stands still. I

guess it's true of any convenience store, really, at least the chain stores with the bright fluorescent lights and the prepackaged miniature versions of everything. I could stare at a tiny packet of Oreos for hours, marvel at the pre-made sandwiches and the Stew In a Bubble (it comes with a fork *and* a straw), and all the magazines with boobs, guns, and cars on the covers. And newspapers I've never seen anywhere else: *The Serbo-Croatian Siren*, *The National Bugle*, and *The Republican-Democrat Advocate* (that last one makes me smile). There's everything here, just not enough of it. There was even a live feed from the Qool Mart's internal network on the security monitor, which the staff was too busy watching to greet us when Mom and I walked in. The left half of the screen was security cam footage from Port Jameson, in fuzzy, elongated, black and white; the right half was in color, and featured Qool Mart CEO Rolland Hoyt standing in front of a featureless background painted with Qool Mart's distinctive reddish-brown color. He was speaking; no audio was being piped out of what he had just called a "renegade franchise."

"...this renegade franchise will be isolated, its assets frozen, and its communication logs heavily scrutinized. The Qool Mart family has always held that—" he raised his hands and flicked his fingers to make them quotation marks— "'going independent' would cause harm to our brand, to our trademarks, to our trade secrets, and most importantly, to the mutually beneficial relationships Qool Mart Co. cultivates with its franchisees.

"To this end, we are insisting that the Qool Mart family pull together in this, the time of our greatest challenge. Please stay open, stay friendly, serve your customers as if they too were a part of your family...of our family. And if any franchisee has any information that could be useful in any way toward engendering a resolution to this crisis, please contact us via the internal network immediately. We'll also be combing through the records of all employees who may have a connection to the Port Jameson store, and would appreciate the full cooperation of all our franchisees and associates to facilitate this matter.

"And finally, we have ordered an air strike on the Port Jameson store. We'd like to make it absolutely clear that this is a private response. The US government is not a part of this operation, though it has allowed use of its air space for the event. Indeed, our insurer, Bell, Winston, and Associates, has taken care of all the incidentals, from selecting the contractors to the sale of ancillary rights for overseas markets. We will also be releasing a one-shot magazine commemorating the forthcoming tragedy, called *Freedom's Qool*, which will be our periodical upsell for November of this year.

"Peace be with you all, and good night and good service."

Randall Hoyt was moved offscreen by a wipe, and a black and white King Daniel eating a hot dog filled the screen. Mom's face burned cold, the way yours does when you almost fall down a long flight of steps, or when a car whizzes by too close. The connection to the god in her temporal lobe faltered for a moment, but then reasserted itself with all sorts of goodie-good chemicals. Everything was going to be okay. Nobody would really blow up a Qool Mart, least of all Qool Mart itself, and if it did, nobody in the store was going to be hurt. They'd get out somehow, or something would happen that would save the day. And gosh, she was right, because back at the store, Rich had just received the news about the imminent attack from Levellin Inc., the manufacturers of Stew In a Bubble, Cherry Bomb Cola, Sweet and Sour Soup Mix, and Cuebars. Levellin shares an insurer with Qool Mart, and someone at Levellin headquarters in England had just received a phone call asking for a "thumbnail guestimate on a going-present basis" about how much inventory might be lost if, say, a Qool Mart was taken out in one shot by an attack copter.

Pardon me, Richard heard in his ear plug, *if it's not too much trouble, could you begin to wrap up programming this evening and bring the camera outside, and beyond the parking lot as well? Thank you very much. We're anticipating an imminent violent incident and we'd prefer that you're not hurt and our property not damaged. Thank you very much in advance.*

My mother snapped, "Stop staring, Herb!" Then she smiled, God's own child again. "You're such a little daydreamer. Been through so much. Why not see if they have an ice cream you like? Or an ice pop? Whatever's less sticky."

"Okay."

"Well, whatever you want!"

To the back of the store I went. Geri kept an eye on me and an eye on the screen, and saw Richard rush up to my father and knock a hotdog out of his hand. Arms started flailing, jaws dropped, Whiting tried to rush the counter and tackle Musad, but Umer jumped on his back, sending them both tilting over onto the display case. Lottery tickets fluttered like moths across the lens of the camera. Adrienne ran off screen toward the doors. Jake punched Richard in the side of the head, and Barry rushed into the middle of it all, trying to hold everyone apart. Then everyone seemed to turn on him. My mother couldn't watch anymore; all the slapping and bumping was damaging her brand new worldview.

I wasn't ready for any more of this either. Instead of the ice cream freezer I went to the stand up fridge that held all the milk, opened the door, and held it open by using a big gallon jug as a doorstop. Then I took out all the other gallon containers, sat on the floor, and sort of wiggled my way under the bottom shelf. It was a tight squeeze, but I was able to turn around onto my stomach and pull the gallon jugs back in. The employees and my mother were so entranced with the screen, and then, with their own dumb conversation—"Say, are you on TV?" "Well, sometimes, but maybe you saw *USA Today* yesterday? I'm Geri Weinberg. You're probably thinking of the front-page article, but I have to say that all those nasty things I said I no longer agree with. You see, I've found G-..."—that they didn't notice all the jostling or even my grunting. The door closed when I pulled that first jug into the freezer after me. Qool Mart uses those great big coolers that are loaded from the back end, not the entrance, so I was able to shift onto my side and stand up, then push open the back door to the unit with my butt. I was alone in the dusty, cold, storage/loading area at the back of the store.

The best part was that once my mother noticed I was missing, she went so crazy that she had to be sedated. The cops were everywhere: running slow with their high beams on to see if I was walking down the shoulder of the highway, checking the little wooded areas between housing developments, knocking on doors. A few of them had even taken the two Qool Mart employees—white kids with pimples and that dumb haircut everyone has—back to the precinct for a beating, in case they were Satanists or child molesters and working with "the enemy."

Nobody bothered to check the storage area. I drank an orange-strawberry-banana juice from a little container that came with its own straw and pulp strainer, and waited. I had a Qool Mart all to myself, my own little nation for a change. Herbia.

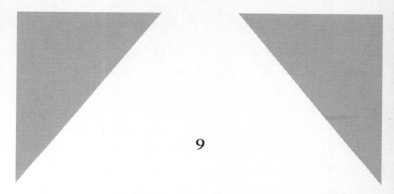

9

In Herbia, I finally felt free. And also chilly. But I remembered hearing on TV once that in the Middle East, old Arab traders were said to drink piping hot tea under the desert sun so that their internal and external temperatures would equate, so I tried the same with some ice pops. It's good to be king. I promised myself that I'd never be extradited. I still wasn't happy, though.

There was one cop car idling outside the store, but the whole place was otherwise abandoned. I'm small enough to not be seen over the counters, and I knew exactly where the junior officer in the car would be looking, and when, so I was able to just walk around the corner, through the Employees Only door, and into the Qool Mart proper, to grab some sweatshirts to use as blankets, and a few comics and magazines to keep myself busy. I also grabbed a flashlight, and a fistful of candy bars. Then it was back to Herbia, and back to my meditations.

At the Port Jameson Qool Mart, things had not gone well. Adrienne was sitting on her butt, moaning, having tripped and fallen, her head hitting the edge of a newspaper rack. Jake's arms were wrapped around my father's belly, while Dad was trying to cough up yet another hotdog-based peace treaty. Richard was screaming that an attack was imminent and that something had to be done. Whiting and the two representatives of the Muslim Republic were wrapped up in one another's limbs, and it sort of fell to Barry to handle things. He had a genius stroke and called Weinbergia.

"Weinbergia," said Kelly on the other end of the phone.

"Is there anything about us on the news?" Barry asked.

"Lemme check," said Kelly. She shouted at the din behind her and sighed the words, "Commercial commercial reality show," before saying, "Ah! No, you're not. Even we're not."

"Uhm—"

"That's bad," Kelly explained. "They must be planning something. Uhm, let me call you back, okay?" Before Barry could say "No, wait—" or offer his eternal love or to lead an escape, she hung up.

Then she decided to talk to me. *Herb?* I heard from nineteen hundred miles away. Kelly was walking up the steps, then pushing her way into my old room. It had become a mini-workshop, full of sawdust and solder—Dad had had the idea to make little garden gnomes with glowing red eyes, to sell as folk art over the Internet—but nobody was on shift at the moment.

Herb? she thought again. *Can you hear me?*

I'd never heard anyone address me directly telepathically before. Well, not and expect me to answer. Sometimes in school I'd pick up something like "Hey, dipshit! Don't take the last lime Jell-O," on somebody's mind. And I wouldn't, but I would "accidentally" poke my thumb into it instead while reaching for a pudding.

I don't know if you can "talk" back to me or anything, but

I've read your little notebook…you know the one, you stopped keeping it a long time ago. You were eight, but you didn't write like an eight-year-old. You described how your parents were thinking, how you could hear people in your head, and you even know what was on people's mind when they thought in other languages.

I figure you're either really creative, need some kind of mental help, or…you're telling the truth.

Can you hear me?

Now I had to scramble for the phone. Another pair of cops had pulled up to the Qool Mart parking lot too, having gotten tired of searching the highway for me. Plus, the Scrapple Apple Pies (pork and MacIntosh, it's like an Easter dinner and dessert in your mouth!) were unguarded. A combination of the easy instincts of the police and pure dumb luck brought the new pair of police into the store and off to different corners where they could see every inch of the shelf space at once.

I hope you can. Something bad is going to happen. Hahaha, I said "going to." Like things haven't been happening already for months now, years. Damn damn, Kel, shut up. He wrote about this sort of blather in his dia—Herb, can you just ignore this part? Delete. Off the record. God, if you can hear me, can you tell me what's going to happen? What should I do?

The police, two young guys whose thoughts were all coffee buzz cut by the natural soothing qualities of a Qool Mart, dawdled over the products, just as I had an hour or so before. They were grooving to logos and bug-eyed mascots, and the occasional whiff of coffee or cheese floating in the air-conditioned breezed, the way you might half-listen to the radio or a CD full of waterfalls to go to sleep. But in the back of their heads, there was a sharpness. Always ready, always watching. I couldn't leave Herbia. No free trade for me, I was trapped behind my own borders, surrounded by belligerents with popular, if incomprehensible, ideologies. They thought I hated them, but they were the ones who hated me. All of them. Even my mother Geri. Even Dad, King Daniel I of Weinbergia. Kids are such a burden, and never quite work out the way you want them to. We're like pets meet really nice cars—you want to show them off, take care of them, own them, get and give affection, but there is still that massive chain of obligation, one that is one-way. Kids don't rush into burning buildings or bust up meth labs for the sake of the police, that's for sure.

It was getting hard to hear Kelly too, because my mother had managed to find a TV camera to put herself in front of, and now a million people were praying for me. I decided to do a kid thing. I squeezed out the back of the freezer, into the storage area, found the circuit breaker box, and flipped the big switch. There was cursing and the sound of fruit pies hitting the floor and then the flashlights went on. The cops headed to the Employees Only door to find the box while I walked back around to the cold room and slipped out under the bottom shelf of the milk fridge to the main part of the Qool Mart, claimed a calling card and a disposable cell phone in the name of Herbia, and then left the store to make a few calls.

"Hello, may I speak with Kelly please?" I affected as deep a voice as I could, holding my chin against my collarbone and speaking through my nose.

"Hey, is this Herb? Where are you, man?" It was one of those smelly guys from Vermont who had recently emigrated.

"I'm right outside the Qool Mart. Can I speak with Kelly please?"

"Aw, that's wicked. You're back with your dad—" I knew he'd jump to that conclusion, and then be happy enough to obey a child. "Sure, let me find Kelly. So, how's it goin' over there? Get any Cuebars?"

"Plenty for everyone," I said. "Listen, could you do my dad one more favor?"

"Sure, anything."

"Go get the gnome and bring it inside."

"Uh, why?"

"State secret. Need to know basis. You don't need to do it if you don't want to. I bet Kelly'll do it. But find her first, and if you do want to do your duty, be sure to keep it a secret, even from Kelly."

"No sweat, li'l dude," he said, then he shouted for Kelly.

"Hi," said Kelly softly.

"Hi."

"So it's—"

"—true," I finished.

"Are you going to—"

"—finish your sentences every time, as proof? No. And red with white lace trim. And you came up with the idea from that old *Superman* movie. And yes, I do think it's a little dirty to make a kid think of an adult woman in her underwear."

"So, what should I do?"

"There's going to be a helicopter attack on the Qool Mart. I'm not sure what to do," I told her. "But if you want to leave Weinbergia, you're going to have a chance. I know a lot of the soldiers are redeploying themselves along Route 25A because Dad left, but there are still a few hanging around."

"Yeah..." she said, tentative.

"Well, there's going to be a distraction. You can probably run over to Tommy Case's house without anybody noticing."

And then, in the tinny distance I heard over the phone some distant yelping and thumps. A soldier had spotted Curtis, the guy from Vermont, making a move for the bomb, and shouted "Hey, he's grabbing the gnome!" and a half-dozen buck privates ran across the border and onto the lawn to tackle and beat him down.

"Thanks!" Kelly said, and she ran out the back door of Weinbergia, the cell phone of state still in hand. She didn't run to Mister Case's, though she was thinking that she would, so she could watch some TV and stretch out on a carpet and have a drink of water and talk to someone without another thirty people breathing down her neck and interrupting and chewing loudly and guffawing at just the wrong moments. But as Kelly crossed the lawn and turned the corner, and saw the yellow and blue glow of the Cases' TV through the bellied-out mesh of their back screen door, she choked on some bitterness in her throat, and ran toward Route 25A.

She wasn't stopped, and didn't even meet any military traffic, except for trucks and occasionally a small brace of soldiers hoppin' to it on foot away from the Qool Mart. Down

Valley Street to the port of Port Jameson, and the ferry to Connecticut. Out to Riverhead or even the Hamptons. One guy, a sniper painted dark and covered in a netting strewn with leaves, lowered himself off the high branches of a tree, and waddled, almost bow-legged, across Kelly's path, crossed Route 25A, and disappeared into someone else's tree-heavy lawn.

Kelly ignored the sign reading CLOSED and rapped at the door. Adrienne looked at her, eyes wide and face pale except for the big egg yolk bump on her temple. *My friend*, Adrienne thought, *whose side is she on now?* Kelly was just happy to see that Adrienne had decided that a knot was better than a steaming crater with its own parking lot, and she pointed at the handles of the door, pantomiming her request to be let in.

"Hey, it's not sound proof or anything," Jake called out. Dad nodded to Kelly as grandiosely as a man with two hot-dogs in each hand could, and Barry took it as a signal to remove the broom and let her in.

"You guys, there's gonna be—"

"—a raid!" Whiting called from the back of the store. He and Umer were huddled by the toys section, filling plastic rockets with a mix of liquid soap and lighter fluid. Kelly hadn't even smelled a thing till she saw the bottles. "A helicopter, probably. Doubt it'll be a Blackhawk or anything of recent vintage, if it's even American."

"I thought the US was attacking?"

"No," Adrienne said. "They're just *letting* it happen to us."

"I find your lack of faith...disturbing," Jake said to Adrienne.

"We should really just evacuate," Richard said. "Cuebar is very serious about this."

"We're being attacked by Cuebar?"

"No, by my own erstwhile business partners," said Musad. Like my father, he was looking grandiose.

"Got it!" Dad said, happy but with clenched teeth. He had another piece of paper between his lips. He handed off the remaining hot dogs to Barry, and unrolled the paper to read it. Another treaty. Peace, in perpetuity, between all of Islam (why not?) and Weinbergia and all affiliates, co-thinkers, and well-wishers.

"This one, I'll sign," said King Daniel.

"That treaty ain't worth the paper it's written on," said Whiting as he gathered up the last red plastic rocket. "Or the hotdog it came out of." Umer, his own arms full of the thin hand pumps that served to pressurize the water kids would fill the rockets with in more peaceful times, nudged him forward.

"You guys seemed to be working together okay," Dad pointed out.

"It's all our necks."

"Ours as well," said Musad. "Thus, the treaty." Whiting snorted and stomped up to the counter to grab a handful of matchbooks and Umer reached up to snag a small vial of Krazy Glue, then the pair walked through the Employees Only door to head to the roof and set up their anti-aircraft battery.

"Can that actually work?" Kelly asked.

Barry shrugged and said, through a mouthful of hotdog, "Well, apparently Omar's grandpa shot down an Apache with a rifle or something, once upon a time."

"Umer," said Musad.

"Whatever," said Barry.

Then came the heavy beating of a rotor twisting through the air.

Hey, Kelly thought to me. *I guess this was a dumb idea all along.* I was tempted to call her again, but I know she wanted a monologue, and that she wished I was able to fortell the future and not just read minds, but I can't. If I could, I wouldn't be in my own personal mess now, telling you all this, would I?

It's pretty different than what you heard about on the news, huh?

Anyway, Kelly thought *I don't want to cry. I know that if I look at Adrienne, I'll start to cry. We were just friends, you know. Not even all that close. We were bored at work, and just wanted to be, I dunno, famous or something. Important. Part of history, whatever you call it. Like you are, Herb.*

I feel so bad. I can't even look at her; she probably hates me for that too now. Kelly started crying. Barry moved, arms wide, to hug, but she jerked away. Everyone stared. Jake shrugged. She ran to the Employees Only door and then up the stairs to the roof, where Umer, Whiting, and the two other employees (both named Mohammed, their name tags reading *Mel* and *Johnny*), who had climbed up the service ladder on the side of the pillbox building to man the spotlight, were setting up. Kelly couldn't see the helicopter, but it was getting close. She was giddy with fear, like that burst of cold sweat when the dentist stops smiling and goes "hmm." Would the store fall to flaming pieces beneath her, leaving her standing in air for a moment that would feel eternal, until it ended in a yank into the fire? That's all she could think of. Standing around a bunch of convenience store workers whose great idea was to launch toys full of homemade napalm at a leased attack copter didn't frighten Kelly at all. It didn't even occur to her.

My mother, all she could think of was me. Me, and making sure that everyone else in the world was also thinking of me. Was I in the grip of some foreign power, like the Palauvians, or was a new country born around me in a windowless brown van with mud over the license plates...a van-shaped country with no age of consent laws?

"Herbie, my darling, my love, my life," my mother told talk show host August Hickey over a cracking telephone line. You probably remember it: Hickey woebegone and staring into his mug while a map of the world pulsed behind him. A still of my mother, in black and white, with her fingers tucked awkwardly under her chin; a shopping mall glamour shop stripped of color for purposes of dramatic import, in the corner. LITTLE PRINCE LOST scrolling horizontally across the bottom of your TV screen.

The copter was a white and red light in the sky.

"There it is, boys," Whiting said, the captain in him asserting himself. Let's stagger the launches. Umer, you'll launch that green number in your hands there as a tracer, then Mel can hit it with a second battery. Johnny, you man the spotlight, try to dazzle 'em. Qool Mart will probably come in low and strafe first, try to scare us, so we have a shot. And if your volleys all fail, I'll use my rocket." He paused, purposefully, dramatically. "For the killing blow."

Mel said, "Oh-kay." Johnny was already busy cleaning moths out of the bowl of the spotlight. Umer just started pumping his rocket.

"I know you can hear me," my mother said to the world, hoping I'd overhear.

Oh, I could.

"I'm sure he can hear me, August."

August nodded, "I am too. We're all praying that your son is somewhere out there, where he can hear you."

"Herb, please, be very careful. And whoever out there has my son, my son, Herb, please, let him go, bring him back home to his mother. I love him so much. Herb has been through just so much recently. He doesn't have a father figure in his life, no male role models. He doesn't know how to survive on his own."

I did wish that I had snagged some jerky or something before leaving the Qool Mart; I just didn't think of it. But with my luck I probably would have been caught somehow, and then I'd have to bring it back and apologize to the store manager or maybe even to Randall Hoyt, who was planning on killing my father.

My father, who was on the verge of a religious experience of his own. Not just head injuries, but stress and nitrates cause religious experiences. Also, believing your own press releases. Dad had all that going on, and the sound of winged death ("winged death"—he actually *thinks* like that sometimes) right outside, so he flipped.

"Musad," he declared, arms thrown wide. "Barry, Jake! Embrace! We are changing the world forever, finally and peacefully."

"Oh, let me get this," Richard said, cam back in his hands, to his knees and then back up trying to get a good angle. Musad put out his arms gladly, Jake laughed and offered one arm to remain heterosexual, and Barry sighed and patted all available backs, careful now to turn his face and avoid the camera.

"Adrienne, come on, join the crew," said my father. "They're afraid of us. The army, the government, big business. We're a threat to them," Dad said. Once again, it was good to be king. "What do you call 'em, Musad, the Great Satan?"

"Nooo," said Musad. "Imperialists, I guess. Not every Muslim believes whatever some mullah in Iran says."

"This is ridiculous," Adrienne said. "I'm leaving."

Jake snorted. "You can't leave. They'll kill you."

Barry said, "Or lock you up in Gitmo and throw away the key."

"No," my father said. "She can go. We're all our own country now. She's safe. You can't imagine America continuing after this. I mean, everyone knows the jig is up. Things will never be the same!" He turned to the camera—it's one of those things people do when they have religious experiences, try to spread the word with the power of eye contact—and said, "Don't you think? Haven't things changed for you out there?" He glanced up, at Richard. "And you?"

"Well, I think we should leave."

"So why don't you go, Richard?" asked Jake.

"C'mon!" said Adrienne.

"I guess I just want to see how this all ends," Richard said. "It's almost like being a journalist or something."

"It's going to end with us all dying!" said Adrienne. "Mark my words—"

"—Oh relax," my father interrupted. "Nothing is going to happen."

Then three bodies flitted into view and hit the parking lot, hard.

My mother sobbed, half for me, half as a way to fill the air while thinking of what else to say to all of you out there in televisionland. Finally she said, "I don't know what else to say, August. I just feel that there is a lot of love out there in the world, and that love is the most powerful force in the universe, and I just hope that everyone prays for everything to turn out okay. I just want everything to be back to normal."

Deep in August Hickey's lizard mind, the old high school reporter who wished that someone would give him the nickname "Scoop" or at least take him seriously, stirred. Dare he ask a follow-up question, instead of just letting this inane woman go on about prayers and love and her snot-nosed brat son, who's probably already in a goddamn ditch somewhere like all these kids always end up being? (Hey!) The hell with it, why not?

"By back to normal," August asked, his tongue and lips no longer even used to the idea of responding to a statement with a question, "do you mean back on Long Island, with your husband? No more countries, no more nuclear crises, no more martial law or garden gnomes or any of that, just back where you were in September?"

Whiting stood triumphant. His shoulders ached, he may have pulled something, he thought, but it was an honest injury. And those Muslim bastards didn't even land on their heads, so it's not like he killed anybody.

"You killed them!" Kelly shouted. *Dead, dead, dead* burned into her brain to the beat of the approaching copter. It was almost soothing in a way; she was hollering only to be heard.

"Ah, they're fine," Whiting shouted back, dismissively waving a rocket. "Fine as those little bastards need to be. Now, let's get that spotlight ready; we'll signal for a pickup, leave the terrorists downstairs, and then my boys'll take care of them."

"We can't do that!"

"You wanna die with the rest of 'em? Go ahead—"

"—but the plan, the rockets."

Whiting tossed Kelly the rocket he'd been holding. "Plastic toys filled with lighter fluid and soap? Good luck, dear." He stomped past her to the spotlight on the other end of the roof, just as the wind of the copter hit the roof hard. The pilot turned on the copter's own floodlight and washed the roof blind.

"Hello!" said a voice, amplified and crackling. "Are either of you Qool Mart employees?" Then the greeting and question were repeated robotically in Arabic. Then in Farsi. In Urdu.

"Yes!" called out Whiting.

"No!" shouted Kelly.

"They're going to save us," Whiting hissed.

"They're gonna blow up the building, why would they save us?"

"Attention Qool Mart employees. Your employment has been as of this moment terminated by order of the Qool Mart board of directors. This means that your employee insurance has been cancelled. This decision may be appealed by submitting an appeal request within sixty days to the Global Arbitration and Mediation Association."

Again the statements were repeated with the weird microchip tinge of a computerized translation and when the third translation was finished, the copter spun so that its side was parallel with the front of the store, the door slid open a man holding a rocket-propelled grenade launcher and wearing a traditional Qool Mart blazer—except no name tag and no little hat—poked out from the interior and took aim.

Kelly planted her feet, wound up, and threw the toy rocket into the wind. It clunked off the edge of the RPG launcher, split open, and spun liquid fire in an arc over the man's head and into the copter. The copter lurched and the computerized voice started again, but squealed hysterically like an old record being played at the wrong speed. The guy fell back and into the bright orange sheet of flame on the far wall of the helicopter, not thinking anything at all but "Whoa!" as he dropped the RPG launcher, which hit the parking lot, bounced hard once, twice, and then didn't go off. The copter, spewing white and black smoke, roared and tore upwards over the rooftops of Port Jameson.

Whiting stared at her, aghast. Kelly said, "Softball. Three-year varsity." Then she cracked her knuckles.

Things seemed to happen very quickly from inside the Qool Mart. Umer and the Mohammeds tumbled into view and lay on the ground, not altogether still. Wind from the helicopter's rotors picked up trash and sand and junk from the parking lot and painted the windows in brown and the flashy reds of newspaper coupon pages. The announcements were made.

"That's not a very good translation," Musad commented.

"Oh, the humanity," Richard said, bending down again and tilting his little camera to take a shot of the underbelly of the helicopter.

"Is there a basement?" asked Jake. "Another entrance somewhere?"

Barry and Adrienne looked toward my Dad, both of them like kids desperately sure that the big man in their life could solve any problem.

"History's on our side," he said.

"Does that mean you have a plan?" Barry asked.

Adrienne answered first. "No, it means that he doesn't care whether or not we die anymore!"

Dad only smiled. Then the copter flared, and the RPG launcher fell, and bounced. Everyone gasped, and even Dad twitched a bit. It bounced again. Barry felt his consciousness sliding down into the core of his spine. Then it settled, and hadn't fired. Umer got his knees and gave a thumbs up. Then, from the back of the store, there was a yelp and half a dozen sharp thuds, and a few more yelps.

Richard swung his camera, and the others all ran for the Employees Only door, from which the sound had come. Musad held up a hand. They weren't employees. He opened

the door and in the tiny vestibule where the door to the restroom was shut and the one to the roof was flung open lay
Captain Whiting on his back, his face dipped in deep red
blood and his nose smashed up against his face. Kelly walked
down the steps and explained, "Tae Kwon Do. Six years."

Somehow my father decided that he was entirely responsi-
ble for all of this. Kelly didn't help when she walked up to
King Daniel, spread her arms and said, "I get it now. I really,
really do. We can do anything we want, anything we need to.
That's real freedom."

Kelly stopped thinking to me. She stopped thinking *of* me.
And so did my dad.

My mother didn't know what to say, or even what to think.
The last dregs of her religious experience melted away, leaving her at a total loss. The whole thing hit her at once: no
fame, no God, no marriage, no child, a public spectacle and
possibly even exposed to harmful amounts of radiation.
That's her life. Geri's life, the girl with the big blonde wings
in her high school yearbook, the former Realtor, the woman
who likes to dip Double Stuf Oreos into her tea because it
makes her feel like a kid and an adult at the same time.

Is Daniel having an affair? was the first coherent thought
to emerge from the fog, even as Hickey was desperately asking follow-up after follow-up now, just to avoid doing something other than staring silently off into the distance. "Do
you hate the people of Weinbergia? Have you found another
man, like the tabloids say? What about Muslims, are they
behind all of this, you think? Are you a Christian? What's the
last thing you said to your son? What were you doing at a

Qool Mart one hundred and ten miles away from your home tonight? Do you think your son is dead? What will you do if Herbert is dead?!"

My mother pictured me dead, face white, eyes wide and still like they were painted plastic, a bit of blood on the lip. Leaves and kicked up dirt everywhere around me, limbs bent exactly the wrong way at elbows and knees. Like the men named Mohammed in the parking lot, but without groaning, no movement, no dizzying replays of the world slipping out from under my feet and bonking me on the head. Seeing her thought was like looking at a photo of myself, or a videotape, more than half blind because not only could I not read any thoughts of myself, but there's nothing there at all, not a twitch or a spark of anything, just me, but no!

"NO!"
Except without even that no.

But that no is what you heard from me, the first time I shouted rather than listened, three days ago. I didn't know that I was able to transmit thoughts, to do anything other than eavesdrop on the world all at once.

As it turns out, I can. My nose starts bleeding, my head feels like two Mack trucks smacked into either side of it, I fall down, and I wake up starved and cold a day later when it rains on me. It took a couple of days to get the new ability under control; it was like bicycling with the training wheels off. I didn't want to clue my parents in to where I was, and I think I might have caused a couple of traffic accidents over on the highway just from thinking, "Shut up, shut up, SHUT UP!"

but now I can do it. Telepathy is much easier now.

So.

So, here we all are then.

10

There are one or two things I know. Reading minds isn't the same as knowing everything, even though I can pick up a lot. Language isn't an obstacle, words are just wrapping paper—you know whether you get a hockey stick or a pair of socks for your birthday based on the shape of the toy or the box; it doesn't matter what design the paper is. But still, some things are unrecognizable. I don't know what the big sigma on some math equations is good for, or what epistemology is or how ambergris was turned into perfume or why Amish people stay Amish or anything like that.

I mean I know what people *think* about those things, when they think it, but that's all. Seeing the hockey stick and playing hockey are two different things.

But, like I said—like I've *been* saying, I know a few things. I said my Dad wasn't crazy when he founded Weinbergia, and it's true, he wasn't. He is *now*, but that's just another thing I know. I know that I need to grow up. It happens to almost everyone eventually; you look at your parents and you see their mistakes, or you bury them and go through their stuff afterwards and you see the gaps: the passport with no stamps on it, because they never made it overseas thanks to all the terror alerts and wars—or just because they liked dreaming on their couch with a coffee table full of pamphlets better.

Or other things. All over the world. The first time your goatherd father fell down while you watched and hurt himself and cried. When your mother cursed in front of you, and then slapped you across the face for being shocked that she'd said a bad word. The first time you go over to your piggy bank or little stash of money and find that there's less change there than there should be, then you smell the tobacco drifting through the screen windows facing the backyard. And you see this, and you grow up.

It happens. It just usually doesn't involve lots of foreign policy and talk shows and explosions.

You probably know the story. The Weinbergians raided a gas station for Cuebars—well, Richard had an expense account and just signed for them, but Kelly did wave the grenade launcher around—and pushed their way back home with the help of the RPG (Kelly said "ROTC" as she hefted it, but she was really just on a crazy brain chemistry high and had never been anywhere near a gun or anything like that before. She'd kicked a man in the face, and was now all-powerful.) The army let them right back in, having already dismantled the gnome bomb, and replacing the statue exactly as it was before.

Dad guessed this would happen and wanted it to. He was tired of the stresses of living in Weinbergia in the nuclear shadow of his own plans. Commercial endorsements were a much better deal. The next day a squad of elite Special Operators burst into the kitchen, guns high on their shoulders, but Adrienne smiled at them and gestured toward the brand new stainless steel three-door Kelvin Refrigertainment Center from which she had just retrieved an ice bag for the bump on her head. They lowered their guns and took down their face masks to smile and nod at one another. She opened the center door. The camera inside—it clicked on along with the little light—recorded their happy wonderment at the size of the fridge, the rotating cake tray, and the holographic smiley faces that floated over the plastic containers of veggies, sauces, and various leftovers, signaling freshness. One face had a flat-mouthed look...better eat that tortellini soon.

I'm sure you all saw that on TV. You might remember PFC Norris from that episode of *Law & Order* where he played that genius crack addict with Tourette's Syndrome. (He got a haircut.) Richard got in good with a few casting directors in the city. Now Weinbergia is all about product placement—and interdictions of suspected Canadians, whom Dad keeps in the basement and pretends to torture. They're fed well, of course, and have their own TV and free access to the basement's half-bath, which actually puts them ahead of the Weinbergian citizens on the upper floors. But the poor things do have to put up with all sorts of questions about Canada whenever someone comes downstairs to get some rice or find a wrench. "Wait, what do you call those hats again? Tooks? I know you told me yesterday, but I forgot." "So, how do doctors make any money?" "Chocolate Twinkies? You're kidding!" That sort of thing.

And my mother? Well, today you got the blue ribbon in the mail. Yes, Geri had decided to reclaim the blue ribbon for herself, because hers are *light* blue, you know, for "boy," so you'd think of me, and pray for me, and then Geri's Generic God would be compelled to get off His holy duff and hand me over. Plus, all the companies that got to put out logos and offers for flashlight keychains and figurines—one of them is modeled after me at age five, except with huge ink blot eyes—loved the idea and paid some private eyes to find me, and some publicists to tell the TV that there were private eyes looking for me.

Even the Islamic Republic of Qool Mart Store No. 351 got into the act—it's a tax haven and makes meth out of cough syrup, then launders the money through a large commercial bank in the city. You know, for freedom's sake. And it keeps your mortgage rates low.

Needless to say, I'm leaving my parents, the Weinbergians, the cops, the army, the PIs, and anyone else who might come after me right now out of this little conversation. And yes, I know what you're thinking: what if someone else, one of us, tells? Well, go ahead and tell. Who do you think will be more open to the possibility that you're receiving a psychic message from me, complaining about my parents: my born-again-twice-a-day mother and her concussion, or the guy who made himself king of his own living room?

Or you could go to the authorities. You could even prove your claim by telling them that you know that the bomb was removed and replaced with a seemingly identical garden gnome during the Qool Mart Treaty crisis. Enjoy your trip to Cuba afterwards. Or, you could hear me out.

What I want to do is be home. This is not the same as going home, because you can never go home again. (See, I listen.) That's what my folks have taught me—Weinbergia is just America Junior now, a TV show with a flag, a tax shelter where at least they speak English and worry about showering often enough, so it's just like the US. My mother thinks the whole universe is watching out for her. God is the mom and dad who never gets mad, always does the right thing, and who can solve any problem, and make everything feel better.

You know, I never remember thinking that of my own folks. One of my earliest memories was of a hard fever, so hot it hurt to blink. Geri was hovering over me of course, with damp washcloths and plenty of juice and then ice packs and children's chewable aspirin that were so gross-tasting to me that I puked them up, so I was put in a cold bath with ice and the next round of tablets were melted into the orange juice and fed to me via tablespoon. She looked at me when I drank the stuff, smiled a thin paper smile, and told me that I was a good boy and that everything would be all right. And just as she said that, she thought—and this was the first thought I had ever heard, other than my own—that she had no idea what she was doing, was a horrible mother, and might end up killing this damn kid. She even entertained, for a second, the idea of just burying me in the group courtyard of the garden apartment complex in which we lived at the time, in case I did die, because she didn't want her own mother to find out if anything ever happened to me. It was just for a second, but she thought it, and she didn't utterly expel it from her mind afterwards, but used me in a hole as a way to distract herself from me on the couch. *"What would I tell Daniel?"* *"Good thing Herb isn't in school yet—only a few people will miss him"* *"Does Daniel love me enough to forgive me if something happened—to help dig?"*

So I always knew parents were faking it. Enough of you are anyway to make the whole world a conspiracy against children. You fall right into it after a certain age. One time, in kindergarten, we were on a class trip and my teacher, Mrs. Surgus had some trouble controlling us. It was sunny, the bus had been full of fumes, and it had been a cold winter with a lot of slush but not too much snow, and this April afternoon felt like the first *real* day of spring. Nobody wanted to hold hands as we walked in double-file. We were all big, most of us had turned six, and hands are sticky and the breeze was so nice and there were lots of things to point at, even on the block between where the bus had let us out and the Port Jameson Museum, which featured harpoons, nets, and the actual desk where a judge once sat while he tried suspected witches.

But it was always a cold February day for Mrs. Surgus—yes, I see you out there still, and it's true, it's true, and what I'm about to say isn't the only secret of yours I know, *Eleanor*—so she decided to put a scare into us. She spotted a man in the window of a creaky old building with one of those haunted-house porches, he was a handyman who was fixing the place up a bit to sell, and pointed to him and said, "Behave, or that man'll get you!" and obligingly the man raised his arms, a long screwdriver in his right hand, and howled like an animal. They didn't know each other, it wasn't a plan. It was just two grown-ups acting in solidarity, because they know how important it is to keep kids terrified and obedient. I knew the truth in a way that the other kids could never imagine, and that made me more scared than any of them. You're either part of the conspiracy, or against the conspiracy.

I could tell stories like this all day, but twilight is coming and it's getting cold again. I just want to tell you something, then ask you a favor.

What I have to tell you: the world you're in is not the world you're from. There are two ways to grow up, and it's just that so far everyone's chosen the easy way—just get new parents and do what they tell you. All families are unhappy, but some—Saudi Arabia, Qool Mart, the Mormons, being "in sales"—are more abusive than others. But even unhappy families are made out of happy people. Nearly everyone has some kind of friend, and if you didn't before, you do now. Me! And if you don't like me, at least I'm a conversation starter. You have something to talk to your pretty neighbor or the guy who sits next to you on the bus or the woman in the next cell about.

Hey, are you hearing what I'm hearing?

Yeah! Freaky, huh?

God, I hope he's not messing up some brain surgeon's concentration right now.

Don't worry, I'm not. For some of you, this is just a daydream, or a smell like the doughnuts you ate as a kid, or a paperback novel, or the orange blobs you see when you squeeze your eyes shut, but you're all in this together. We're all in this together. Well, you all are. I'm going to grow up the *other* way. But I need your help. Specifically, I need you to forget, just for a few minutes, everything you think you know about kids and travel and the dangers of the shoulder of the highway and the outstretched arm. I need you to anticipate my coming and do something other than shout at me, "Hey kid, get off my lawn!"

Because I'm going back to Weinbergia.

11

Lenora Cline-McGrath: "Life is a strange and wonderful place, full of the bittersweet and just plain bitter," my grandma always used to say. "But it's the second that makes the first taste better," and indeed, she was one hundred percent right. I like having my own country with Gary. We signed a separate peace treaty too, with about three hundred different countries. Have you seen treatyonline.org yet? It's very handy.

Politically, we argue all the time, but he's pretty open to being educated. He's a passionate man. Ever since the bomb, he's just gotten more passionate. We all have to help each other now, I guess. Of course, it was horrible, a tragedy, nothing will ever be the same, but you just have to keep on living. We're living just fine out here. We're very open now, even single-race couples can emigrate if they wish to, as long as they can pass our citizenship tests. We interview them and if they can get through it without saying "Some of my best friends are…" or "I grew up around…" then they're good.

We do get a fair amount of hate mail, it's true. But that's fine, live and let live. Have your opinion; have your ugly-ass stamps with your cracker grandfather on it, that's fine. We don't care. We're happy now. How many people can truly say that they're happy?

[laughs] Yeah, I know. Everyone is supposed to say that they're secretly happy now, right?

Roger Whiting: I was being debriefed, so that's why I'm alive today. We're lucky—damn sure that *I'm* lucky at least—that there was some concern that I'd turned, so I wasn't present in DC that day. Yeah, by debriefed I mean interrogated, but by interrogated I don't mean tortured or anything. They let me have a coffee, tissues, anything I wanted. About seventeen hours, all told, including the polygraph. It was fine. I'm just glad to be home. I'm still an American. Arizona is full of *normal* people, thank the Lord.

Richard Pazzaro: We were watching TV in the living room when it happened. First the gnome started falling over, then it fell over. Then came the light. That was pretty much it. I know we're not supposed to use the word ironic anymore, but it just seemed, you know, ironic to me that the bomb was being paraded around as some sort of trophy. It was like the Soviet Union or something, wasn't it? Well, they marched their own weapons through Red Square, not captured ones, but if they *had* captured an American nuke or something, I'm sure they would have shown it off.

Jesus Porter (former Secretary of Veteran Affairs): Yeah, we joked about it, my undersecretaries and I. Everyone after the Attorney General in the line of succession does. Even after 9/11, or so I was told. I was still in the private sector then. VA was never a "lesser" department, succession is based on the founding of the particular Cabinet departments.

I didn't return to Washington, but not because I was afraid. Never let it be said that I was afraid. Really, what was there to be afraid of? I was in Burlington, visiting my mother. The city had already "gone indie," as the kids say, but there was an open border and we weren't recognizing any microstates at the time, and really *nobody* was, not even their own so-called citizens. All the stores on Church Street still took American scrip, and that's really the decisive element of the existence of a state as far as I'm concerned. So I was there and I was fine with it, and security was fine with it, and the FBI was entirely fine with it.

I just didn't want to go back. I never wanted to be President. It struck me, walking through the streets after I'd heard, with people gathering around their car radios, others opening up their windows and bringing their TVs to the windowsills, just to let the people hear what was going on...there wasn't panic. There wasn't even much sadness, not once the estimated death counts were dialed down from forty-five thousand to six hundred. And the wind didn't blow the radiation into Virginia or the suburbs. Most of the people I met just seemed relieved, as if an obnoxious uncle had left and the unpleasant Christmas dinner was finally over. So I decided to stay here. I run a little juice stand three days a week. It's nice. I like working with people.

Mirella "Madusa" McAlister: I picked the kid up on the Kansas-Missouri border. He looked fine. Clean, well-fed. I'd heard him. I didn't want to get into trouble, but I didn't want to get him into trouble either. Herb was a polite little man. No, I never wanted children; I barely had a mother of my own, so it wasn't my ovaries talking. We stopped outside Jefferson City for a potty break and next thing I know, I'm in Little Rock and only then did I remember that he wasn't with me anymore.

Adam Indore: We tracked him for a while. SatMaps.com is really handy. You know, I'm sure. One time, I used it to find a keychain that fell out of my pocket at Burning Man. I had spares of all the keys, of course, but the keychain was a limited edition that came as some swag if you bought a *The Stars My Destination* DVD boxed set on the first day, and I was on the line for three days to get it, so it had a lot of sentimental value. It was really lonely looking out there on the playa by itself. Anyway, I put out a call on all the listservs, and the next year someone snagged it for me and delivered it to Camp The But I Love Hims And Other Fake Band Names, which I was associated with that year. So it's a great tool, I highly recommend it.

Anyway, yeah, we were tracking him, and I was using this Tibetan technique I'd picked up at my dojo to blank out my mind so he wouldn't sense my endeavor, but I guess my roommate Todd—and he won't be my roommate anymore after the lease is up, that's for sure—gave it away because after that he'd constantly duck under doorways or walk under the canopy of trees on highway dividers.

Laurel Richards: The numanist community will never be the same.

Kelly Donnor: God, I wish I was famous for *just* fifteen minutes. The books, the PhD dissertations, the *cultists*, they just don't stop. Half of them have me set up as the Virgin Mary to Herb's Jesus, the rest want me to be Mary Magdalene. I used to argue with them, but there's no dissuading true believers. What Herb's message was, I mean, to the extent that he even had a message, is just this: "Grow up!" You're not supposed to be looking for a new mama and a new papa, especially when that new mama is me. Of course, true believers, like I said. How many murders has "Thou Shalt Not Kill" prevented? How many murders have true believers in "Thou Shalt Not Kill" precipitated? Yeah, that's my point.

No, I haven't kicked anyone in the face since that night. After the adrenaline wore off, I found out I tore a tendon. Thank God Weinbergia had a doctor. She was just out of her residency, and she really wanted to help the unfortunate. It was either us or India, and she wanted to be close to a mall. Isn't that a riot?

Herb hasn't talked directly and only to me since that night either, no. I miss him. I haven't talked to Adrienne either. I think she emigrated to Ocean Parkway in Brooklyn. Was she sleeping with Daniel? Ugh, I hope not.

Thomas Case: I don't give two craps. I didn't give two craps before, and I don't give two craps now. You know what "growing up" is? Growing up is getting a job; making sure your kids are fed, healthy, and going to school; and, minding their own business. I just want to live my life. Anything that helps is good. Anything that hurts is bad. I had a lot of civil rights, and they didn't help. I gave some up, it didn't help. My neighbor built a nuke, and that didn't help either, and neither did all those soldiers peeing on my driveway and leaving their cigarette butts everywhere. The whole thing was just disgusting, I tell you. I don't bust my ass everyday to come home to that. People should have some respect. That's growing up!

I want to see what these cooler-than-thou types are gonna do when the Mexicans come swarming over the border, or when there's a hurricane and nobody to fix up their little "country" homes after the flooding.

from **topplethegnome.com**: The "official account" of the events—to the extent that anything emerging from the Georgetown rump can be considered "official"—of 10/19 is full of inconsistencies and even impossibilities, but the media is not interested in seeking out the truth. Take the following into account:

How does a nuclear bomb, even a small, home-brew bomb, manage to detonate after falling onto its side? This has never happened before in the history of the existence of nuclear weapons. Wouldn't the vibrations from the travel from New York to our nation's former capital have set it off? What about the fissionable material that traversed our nation's highways during the Cold War, and the third Gulf War, and the Sino-Sacramento incident?

Why wasn't the gnome secured? Why wasn't the gnome disarmed?

Why, for the first time in recent memory, was there a "parade of spoils" that left the President and so much of the cabinet vulnerable and out in the open?

What about video footage of the "first flash," which was also widely reported by witnesses?

What about "Weinberg Sympathy Syndrome?", the so-called mental disorder widely reported on in the days immediately before the detonation?

THE ANSWERS WILL SHOCK YOU!!

There is only one force on Earth capable of eliminating the federal government of the United States, and that is...the federal government of the United States. Remember that the government is huge, being both the single largest employer and the single largest spender of money in the world. Many layers of government exist "below" the figurehead President and his cabinet-level appointees; these civil servants have frequently been called "the permanent government" by social scientists and other legitimate scholars.

Also note:

Not one of the one hundred and nine Republican Representatives or the forty-one Senators were on the platform or dais at the time of the explosion. Why would they not be in attendance on that fateful day?

Not one member of the Supreme Court was in even Washington DC on 10/19.

The IRS, Federal Reserve, VA, Homeland Security, and FEMA—all elements of the "permanent government"—had "off-capital" offices up and running within hours of the detonation...as if such an attack had been planned for in advance.

FACTS:

Approval ratings for the President were at a historic low of 21% on 10/17.

The government had "shut down" earlier that year due to contentious budget battles in Congress. Without news reports...would you have noticed?

Since the detonation and the subsequent secession trend, the Georgetown Rump government was able to withdraw billions from infrastructure, entitlement, law enforcement and other federal projects. Much of this money has been poured into deficit and debt recovery, enriching foreign creditors with close connections to the various remaining federal departments.

Most of the "new countries" that have emerged in the wake of the Weinbergia secession and then post 10/19 retain American customs, language, tastes and sometimes even our money. They have simply excluded themselves from both taxation and services, allowing a networked underground economy to emerge. A network that actually allows for a number of previously illegal activities to emerge unchecked...but for the profit of the Rump which can now get away with those activities as well!

Think about it. Who has the motive, the means, and the opportunity to seemingly strike a "killing blow" against the American government? The answer is clear: the American government destroyed itself in a public and inexplicable way, in order to consolidate its power: the President and his "bully pulpit" are gone, and now only the pure bureaucratic force of apparatchiks—a bureaucracy much larger and more powerful than is needed to provide "services" to their so-called "citizens"—remain. The Gnomes of Zurich are AMERICAN and they have ALREADY WON!!

Ty Towns, Bargeland: We didn't pick him up, he just showed up, really. I'm not sure how he got onto the barge. Jedi Mind Trick or something? We have lots of dinghies, supplies coming on and off all the time. He could have snuck in on to any of them. Smart kid. Little creepy, though. Funny how he stayed so clean; lots of people must have taken him in for a night or two, let him use the shower, get a good night's sleep on a guest dignitary bed.

Geraldine "Geri" Weinberg was unavailable for comment, on the advice of her lawyers and her spiritual adviser, TV personality Dr. Hamilton Crabb.

King Daniel I, Weinbergia: He came to the door, right after sunset one night. A few of the people in the living room were pretty spooked. We'd been following the news as best we could, of course, and lots of people were very helpful in reporting their encounters to us. I just wasn't sure what was going on—obviously, a lot of the information we'd received was false. People claimed he was dead, that he appeared before them in "ectoplasmic form" (whatever that is), that he was claiming to be the "Holy Grail" and a descendent of Jesus, or a Muslim. We had a big cork bulletin board in the rumpus room with all the sightings, to try and separate the wheat from the chaff.

I wanted to hug him, but my arms just felt heavy, like lead, and I couldn't move them from my sides. I wasn't afraid or anything; after all I'd been through in trying to get this country off the ground, I think the fear centers of my brain had burnt themselves out. But I couldn't move, and I knew he had something to do with it.

"Dad," he said, "just listen." And he talked for a while, about being a grown up and what he thought it meant. It was kid stuff mostly, *Catcher In The Rye*-style preciousness, but he really thought he was on to something. Heh, I dunno. Maybe he was at that. Basically, I guess he just sees that when people are patriotic, when they care about a society that's greater than themselves, when people find what they have in common with others and form nations, that they're somehow pathological or neurotic to do so. He said that the solution to imaginary lines wasn't more imaginary lines. That "vertical formations" don't work, whether they're families or countries.

I wanted to tell him, "Hey, how far do you think you would have gotten if it wasn't for me making sure your little butt was wiped and there was food on the table?" but I couldn't say anything. I didn't like that, but then it occurred to me that I'd, and plenty of times, made him stand in a corner and be quiet while I lectured him about proper behavior. Is that how it feels? I guess I remember that queasy stomach feeling from when I was a kid too, but I got over it.

I was proud of him, though, because he thanked me. Lots of kids his age would fire back with "I never asked to be born!" or something as juvenile. He said he was very grateful to be raised by a man like me, by someone who "almost got it." I guess I've said I've never asked to be born American, eh? Yeah, he pointed that out too me, as if he could read my mind. But the final trick is to ask what you *were* born to be, and to be that thing.

Then he disappeared. No, he didn't run off, he disappeared. I realized then that after he was kidnapped, I'd really stopped thinking about him. Affairs of state got in the way. I missed him, but he was with his mother, and really, the border wasn't the best place for a child. My great-great grandmother sent her son to America long ago, so he'd be safe from the pogroms, so it was sort of the same thing…wasn't it?

Qool Marts are different now. There are a lot more weird things on the shelves, like homemade taffy from some old lady's country down the block. In another store, a few miles and two border stations away, it's all misshapen cookies with vanilla and chocolate frosting. One of the ones Rich and I stopped at on our whirlwind tour even had real stew, and benches to sit at, and corn bread. They took out the hot dog machines and microwaves and turned the front of the store into a picnic area. It's pretty nice, but uneven. Sometimes I miss being able to walk into any Qool Mart or McDonald's or whatever and being sure that every bite and every glance would be exactly the same. Sort of like bathrooms in the suburbs I've walked through.

Also, sometimes the new Qool Marts just throw rocks at the car when they see us coming.

We got some plastic sunglasses and ice cream sandwiches—a local brand where the sandwich part actually tastes like chocolate, maybe even too much like chocolate. But it beats the old industrial confection: an inert substance designed to have the peculiar texture and flavor of not-quite-right-but-inoffensive. Richard had the camera. We paid with exposure on our feed, except for the gas. A pile of various local monies did that trick.

In the car, Richard put the cam on the dash and said, as he said after every stop, "Where to?"

"I dunno," I said. "Canada?"

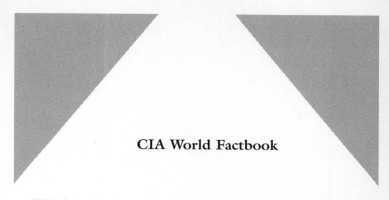

CIA World Factbook

Weinbergia

Background
The first of the modern "armed micronation" trend, Daniel Weinberg built a nuclear device in 20—and seceded from the United States. Open "borders" into the fledgling state and a custody case led to a tense standoff between Weinberg and the United States, which was resolved when the nuclear device was captured without incident. The device later accidentally detonated in Washington DC.

Geography
Location: Divided lot on North Shore of Long Island.

Geographical Coordinates: 40 N 56 ,73 W 03

Area: 40" x 200"

note: includes home of 20" x 50"

Area Comparative: One third of one city block (Washington DC)

Land boundaries:

total: 480"

border countries: United States 480"

Coastline: —

Environment current issues: lice infestation from "refugees"

People

Population: no indigenous inhabitants

note: Approximately thirty-seven individuals, thirty-two of them American citizens, have taken up residence in Weinbergia and have renounced their citizenship. A UN observer (Palau) is also a long-term resident as of 1 December 20—.

Languages: English, "Weinbergian" pidgin.

Government

Country name:

conventional long form: The Kingdom of Weinbergia

conventional short form: Weinbergia.

Dependency status: A sovereign nation, in practice Weinbergia closely adheres to US laws and social mores.

Capital: Living room.

Legal system: King is standing sovereign, with moral suasion and pseudo-consensus driven voice votes among population working as a *de facto* veto.

Executive branch:

chief of state: King Daniel I, Weinbergia

head of government: King Daniel I, Weinbergia

elections: issue ballots with voice votes, as needed.

Diplomatic representation in the US: none

Diplomatic representation from the US: none

Flag description: several models of the flag, some parodic, have been offered. Most common is a dark blue field with an image of Daniel Weinberg at age twenty-three, with sideburns and sunglasses, in the center.

Economy

Economy overview: Economic activity is limited to funding extraordinary rendition, remittances from ideological co-thinkers, "off the back" infusions from new immigrants, and intellectual property (book, reality programming, video game) based on Weinbergian "concept."

Communications

Radio broadcast stations: None. Uses podcast technology.

Television broadcast stations: None. Uses Internet connections to stream media.

Military

Military note: Weinbergia is no longer a nuclear power.

∧ ∧ ∧

Like everything else about this book, these acknowledgments were difficult to write. I started *Under My Roof* in 2003, and completed it on May Day, 2006. It doesn't take three years to write 40,000 words, but it does take three years to studiously not write most of them. I'm sure I'll miss some people then, as it's been a long, hard, trip, but from the top of my head I'd like to thank Richard Nash, Michele Rubin, Tennessee Jones, Eliani Torres, Lynn "Tom" Cully, Brian "Lance" Cully, Chris Bell, Kynn Bartlett, Tim Pratt, Heather Shaw, Jody Sollazzo, Melinda R. Himel, Catelin C. Compton, and Keshet Savin. I began writing this book while living in reduced circumstances on Long Island, but reduced circumstances are better than none. So, thanks to my parents Panagiotis and Rena Mamatas, my sister Teddie Mamatas, my uncle Peter Vroutos, and my cousin Willow Vroutos.

Distant allies include Barbara Ehrenreich and the rest of the staff of and contributors to *Seven Days*, Jonathan Levy who once told me "Read everything, classics and crap. Start with Aeschylus and end with Zola," which lead me to start with Aeschylus and get quickly to Aristophanes, and Reynard Roxbury, who planted the germ of this book twelve years ago with an off-hand comment I doubt she remembers.

If I have forgotten you, please write your name into this copy of Under My Roof in this space: _____ .

Pru Phur

Nick Mamatas is the author of the Lovecraftian Beat road novel *Move Under Ground*, which was nominated for both the Bram Stoker and International Horror Guild awards, the Civil War ghost story *Northern Gothic*, also a Stoker nominee, and over thirty short stories and hundreds of articles. His work has appeared in *Razor*, *Village Voice*, *Spex*, *Clamor*, *In These Times*, *Polyphony*, several Disinformation and Ben Bella Books anthologies, and the books *Corpse Blossoms*, *Poe's Lighthouse*, *Before & After: Stories from New York*, and *Short and Sweet*. By the time this book is published, he'll be living in a different state than the one he lives in now.